# THE GOAT KILLER

Clive Ward

Copyright © 2016 Clive Ward/oneroofpublications.com

All rights reserved.

ISBN-10: 1534696318
ISBN-13: 978-1534696310

# DEDICATION

This book is dedicated to all my former army colleagues.

## By Clive Ward

The Unnamed Soldiers
Army Barmy
Sir Yes Sir
At Home with Kev & Trev
If Babies Could Talk
Drill Pig & Pongo

## Writing with E Ward

Half Day Closing

# ACKNOWLEDGMENTS

I'd like to thank family and friends for their encouragement to write this book. Special thanks go to Matt Milner for his advice on Afghanistan, and my editor, Antonella Caputo for her research and advice.

# CHAPTER 1

'Ladies and gentlemen, welcome to Afghanistan. For the correct local time, please set your watches back three hundred years.' We received this greeting when the plane landed, and our deployment began.

The roar of the two Chinooks faded as they flew off into pitch darkness. There was tension in the air as we watched them leave. It's five in the morning, the temperature was hovering just above freezing. For most of my comrades, all they could think about was getting back in their sleeping bags, which were lying empty back in our patrol base, but not me, I love this shit.

The last couple of weeks we had been busy. In the last twenty-four hours, we had to deal with a suicide bomber, two IED (improvised explosive device) finds and a direct hit on a patrol, but luckily no casualties so far.

We were heading for a suspected Taliban compound a few miles down the road. Just last week a local teenager struck up a friendly conversation with a passing patrol. Having identified the commander, he ambled off to collect his suicide vest from a neighbouring compound, then walked back over to his new 'friends' and blew himself up. The young Taliban recruit failed to take anyone else with him on his suicide mission. Luckily for the commander and his men, there was a delayed reaction, giving them enough time to take cover.

We'd been patrolling for twenty minutes, everyone was focused apart from Daz, as usual. Sometimes, Daz could be a bit of a liability, that's why I was always on his case. I knew it pissed him off, but it was for his own good. All he'd gone on about since we arrived in Afghanistan, was going home, and what he was going to do to his girlfriend, but we all knew he didn't have a girlfriend.

Daz turned round to talk to Matt, 'Cheer up mate, only thirty days to go and we'll be out of this shit hole forever.'

Matt is my older brother. We don't look alike. He is tall and thin, I'm stocky. He is dark haired, while I'm blondish. Sometimes I think my mum slept around. He is the most switched on soldier in the platoon. You wouldn't want anybody else watching you back. Today was different; Matt was walking around with his head up his arse and his mind in neutral.

'You won't be going anywhere Daz, if you don't shut the fuck up. Turn round and keep your eyes peeled, you too Matt.' I glanced my brother's face, he was gloomy, 'What's up Bro?'

'Nothing... just feeling a bit homesick. It's the twins, birthday today.'

Matt was married, he had two girls, only three years old. We'd been here for five months now. I think this place is finally getting to him. Missing the twins' birthday, no wonder he was feeling like shit. Having spent our childhood in care, family was important to Matt. I'd do anything for my brother. I had only one problem, his wife. We shared a mutual dislike of each other. The only time I could see Matt was at work, or on the rare occasions when she let him go on a lad's night out.

Home, it is the last place I want to be. This is my second tour. I love this place. They all think I'm nuts, maybe I am?

## The Goat Killer

When the shit hits the fan most of this lot take cover, but it is when I'm in my element. The adrenaline rush I get from the threat of danger, makes me feel alive.

They nicknamed me M and M, Mental Mickey after my first tour, and it stuck. There's a rumour going around that the SAS turned me down, because I was too crazy, I just let them think that. Yes, I am a bit of a nutter, but I suppose that if I had a family, a wife and kids, things would be very different.

We'd patrolled another two hundred metres and then it happened, *boom*. Someone had stood on an IED. I couldn't remember much after that, I just laid on my back with a mouth full of dust. The next thing I heard was gun fire and panic.

'Get up! Come on Mickey... we've got to get the fuck out of here, there are Taliban everywhere... get up!'

I didn't want to get up, I was happy just lying down there staring at the sky. The sound of the gunfire faded into the background and then it went silent.

'Are you getting up? The alarm went off thirty minutes ago and your coffee's getting cold. I'm not going to call you again.'

What the fuck? It took me a while to come to my senses. It was Debbie calling me. I wasn't in Afghanistan. I was at home in bed. It had been another nightmare, one of many. I got out of bed and showered. Putting my dressing gown on, I made my way downstairs.

'You were dreaming again, weren't you? Don't you think it's about time you do something about it?'

There she goes again, trying to get me to see someone about my nightmares. What can the doctor do anyway? It's not like they can go inside my head and take away the memories.

'I'm bound to have nightmares. You'd have them too, if you'd seen some of the things I have.' But it wasn't just nightmares, it was much more serious than that, and I knew it.

'Where's my coffee?' I said, trying to change the subject.

'It went cold. I'll make you another one,' she said, as she slammed a mug down on the worktop. Debbie was always moody in the morning. Give her a few hours and she'd snap out of it

'I've got to get the kids up later for school, then I've got to go to the doctor and...'

I switched on my electric razor to drown out her bitching. It's become a regular thing now, but all she did, was raise her voice. If I had a pneumatic drill, she'd raise her voice even higher. Same shit, different day. Boy, she can go on and on. She unplugged the razor.

'You're not well Mickey, you need help. If it carries on I'm moving into the kids, room.'

I just looked up at her. We had the same conversation nearly every day.

'I was trying to have a fucking shave.'

'Mickey you're scaring me, you're getting worse. You can dream about what you want, but when it involves me, I draw the line.'

Do we have to have to talk about this, every fucking morning?' I snatched the razor's plug back from her hand, and I put it back into the socket.

# The Goat Killer

'Don't shout you'll wake the kids.'

'What do you mean involving you? You weren't fucking there!' The memory of the nightmare she was talking about, came back to me as clear as day.

We'd set up ambush on this track, because we'd had a tip off that a Taliban patrol would be heading our way. It was late evening, I was on cut off (ambush position) with Daz, when I heard movement. I looked over at Daz, he'd fallen asleep and was snoring, I had to shut him up. Suddenly I wasn't in Afghanistan and I wasn't in an ambush. I was lying in bed with my left arm wrapped tightly around Debbie's neck, with my right hand covering her mouth.

'Shut the fuck up, don't make a sound,' I whispered in her ear. I looked towards the bedroom window, three figures passed by, silhouetted by the streetlights, they were clearly Taliban carrying AK's. The fuckers were everywhere. Whether it was her elbow digging into my side or something else, the dream was over and I was awake. I knew what she was talking about. The last thing you want, is being woken up by some head case strangling you, in the middle of the night.

Debbie started to cry. That was a new tactic on her part.

'I've had enough Mickey. You need to see someone. You're not the same person since you left the army.'

'Forget it Debbie, I'm not seeing any more shrinks. There's nothing wrong with me, it's just a few bad dreams that's all.'

I was lying. After the incident, which left me with head injuries, they said I was ok, that I'd make a full recovery, but they were wrong. I hid the truth, I might have recovered physically, but mentally I had big problems and I knew it.

I could hide it most of the time. I wanted to get back out there, I wanted to soldier on, I loved the army. I was about to be deployed on my third tour, when the army made me redundant.

I was a boy soldier. I'd joined up when I was sixteen, the army was my life, it was the only life I knew. I was devastated. Yes, I had a reputation in the army for being a bit psycho. If there was a dangerous mission, I would be first in the queue, but now I'm in civvy-street and I can't deal with it. After serving my country for ten years, I was out on my arse. Here's a wad of money, now fuck off, that's what redundancy felt like. What could I do in civvy-street? As far as a job went, all I could put on my CV was professional killer. I can remember the reaction I got at the job centre.

'Is this some kind of joke, sir?'

'Joke, fucking joke. That was my job, just give me a job, I'll do anything,' I said.

'Sir, will you refrain from swearing? If you carry on swearing, I'll have to ask you to leave.'

What was the first job this bloodthirsty, adrenaline junkie, as I am, got offered? Standing on a street corner all day, wearing a fucking box promoting pizza. I don't even like fucking pizza. If only I'd had my SA80 on me at that moment, I'd have blown his fucking head off. He read my CV, he'd been warned.

I stood up and walked over towards Debbie, who was standing at the kitchen sink, staring aimlessly out of the window. I knew she could sense I was behind her, but I did nothing. I wanted to slip my arms around her, but I couldn't show any sign of affection. It was a thing of the past.

'Right, I'm off to work,' I said turning away from her.

It was just after twenty past five in the morning, my shift started at six. I had taken a job as a contract security guard at the local agricultural college, a job that I hated, but it was a job. I knew I wouldn't be there forever.

'Your pack-up's in the fridge, by the way,' Debbie said.

She didn't turn around. I didn't say a thing, just took my pack up and left. There was nothing I could say, our close relationship had ended a long time ago.

## CHAPTER 2

It was the middle of March and spring was in the air. It was nearly daylight and warm for the time of year. I decided to walk the short distance to work. Usually I couldn't walk down the street without worrying something was going to happen, but not this morning. I was out of the house and feeling ok. My problems only occurred in my sleep or when I was under pressure. I knew if I got too stressed, I'd sometimes go into a trance or waking dream. I tried hard to avoid anything stressful while I was at work. I walked down the street mumbling to myself. Debbie's comments had hit a nerve.

'What the fuck's up with her? I'm not the same person, well who the fuck am I then? She's delusional, it's all in her head, I'll show her.' I carried on talking to myself walking down the street. A local resident was out walking his dog and stopped when he spotted me, before quickly crossing the road to avoid me. Anyone would think I'd gotten the fucking plague or something.

It didn't take long for me to collect a reputation, for being a bit of a hard man in the area. I was working nights a few months ago, when some wanker started playing their shit music full blast, at nine in the morning, when I was trying to sleep. I knocked on their door and asked them to turn it down, which they did, but the next day they did it again. So I knocked on the door again. This time when they opened the door, I went straight to where the CD player was, picked it up and threw it out onto the street. Since then, the street has been really quiet.

## The Goat Killer

I walked into the local shop, to pick up my paper and pouch of Golden Virginia. I'd known Nazim, the shop owner, since I was a boy. Nazim Ali originally came from Kashmir, he settled in the UK in the sixties. He ran his shop like clockwork, the paper and baccy were waiting for me on the counter every morning. It's as though he knew my shift pattern, but really he always spotted me coming, Naz didn't miss a thing. He would have made a great informer if he'd been in Afghanistan.

'Morning, Mickey, how are you this morning mucker?'

'I'm fine, nice morning. Who's winning?' I asked, staring at the TV.

There was a cricket match on, there was always a cricket match on. Naz was open seven days a week, from six in the morning until eleven at night. If you needed a pint of milk on Christmas day his shop would be the place to go.

'Nobody's winning until the end, it's a five day, test match.'

'Oh, right. I'll see you tomorrow then,' I said.

I was getting closer to the college, so I rolled a smoke and smoked it quickly, before I got to the college driveway and in range of the CCTV camera's. The college had a strict no-smoking policy. Just then I felt my phone vibrate in my pocket. That'll be a text from Debbie I thought, I bet I've forgotten something or she's leaving me. I checked my phone, it wasn't from her. It was from my girlfriend Chrissie.

"*Hi my big brave, bad ass soldier, will I be seeing you tonight? Or are you still tied up, like I was last week. You, kinky fucker xxx.*"

I didn't reply, I knew it would imply that I was back in the country. I put the phone back in my pocket and carried on walking.

'Morning, Mickey, where's your car?' Derek asked, as I arrived at the gatehouse. The gatehouse was a small building at the top of the driveway, next to the barrier. It was functional rather than comfortable, with a desk, telephone, 2 chairs, a filing cabinet and the CCTV screens. As far as I was concerned, the most important piece of equipment in there was the kettle. The equipment in the gatehouse was outdated and should have been replaced. Out of twenty CCTV cameras on the campus, only eight actually worked properly.

'I walked it.'

'Sod that, I don't walk anywhere.'

'That's because you're a senile old cunt Derek,' I said, laughing.

Derek Warner had just finished his twelve hour, night shift, I was his relief. He took a friendly swing at me, he reminded me of my friend Daz's old man.

'Too slow old man, too slow.'

'It's a good job I know you or I'd knock you out.'

'Of course you would.'

Derek was sixty- six and due to retire the following week. I liked Derek, he was one of the good guys, he'd do anything for you. He'd served twenty-two years in the Signals regiment. I could sit for hours listening to his pull up a sandbag stories, especially his stories about tours of Northern Ireland in the seventies.

'I've made you a cuppa,' he said handing me a mug of tea.

'Cheers, mate.' The tea was as dark as brandy with just a hint of milk in it. It was too strong for me, so I put the mug down on the desk.

The old man picked up my paper and started to read it. He did it every morning when I took him off.

'Dave Sherwood's popping by in a bit, he wants a word,' Derek said.

'What the fuck does he want?'

'Christ knows, probably more bullshit I suppose. He walks around like he's the principal, no one would believe he's only the site manager.'

'I'm here now. Haven't you got a home to go to?' I said looking forward to a few minutes on my own, and a decent cup of tea, before people started arriving.

Derek sat in the corner flicking through the paper. It took him a few minutes to reply.

'I'm waiting for my missus. She's picking me up, we're off to see my son in Birmingham. Didn't I tell you, I'm a granddad again, we're going to see the new baby.'

'How many is that now?'

'Nine.'

Derek had his retirement all planned out, he was going to sell his house and buy a smaller property in the country, then buy himself a camper van, so he and his missus could tour Europe.

'Isn't this your old unit?' Derek pointed at a picture in the paper, 'it says here they're marching through town on Saturday, are you going?'

'No, I'm fucking not. I told you I want nothing to do with them. Ten years I served, then they just kicked me out like an unwanted dog.'

'Maybe getting made redundant was for the best. You didn't want to go back to Afghanistan again, not after what happened to you out there.'

'I told you, I don't want to talk about it. Ok?'

'Enough said. All I'm saying is, you need to sort those demons of yours out, that's all.'

Shit, not again. First, it's Debbie, now Derek. I changed the subject, I was getting sick of the constant nagging from everyone.

'What time's your missus coming?' I asked.

'Any minute now, why?'

'She better hurry up, before I knock your head off.'

Derek started to laugh, 'you and who's fucking army?'

'Morning all.' The site manager David Sherwood called out as he entered the gatehouse.

I had to stifle a laugh, when I saw Derek roll his eyes. He really disliked the site manager.

'Right, I can't stop. I've just popped in to drop this key off,' Sherwood said dangling a key-ring with several keys attached, 'I've padlocked off the old plant sales, greenhouses and the poly tunnels. They are now a no-go area, and it's staying that way until next year. If the college get the building grant they've asked for, then they'll be getting knocked down and a new teaching block built in their place.' He added as if the project was his idea.

Me and Derek call it the compound. The area is about the size of an old football pitch, about a quarter of a mile from the gatehouse, on the border of the college grounds and backing on to the canal. The land it stood on, had previously been part of a farm the college had bought. The compound contained greenhouses, poly-tunnels and two large potting sheds, as well as some large storage buildings. I, for one was glad, that meant we didn't have to patrol it. Dave Sherwood carried on with his bullshit. The drone of his voice began sending me to sleep. I started to drift into one of my dream like states. Sherwood suddenly turned into my ex platoon commander who was briefing us.

'*Until then nobody is allowed in there unless they have my permission. If we do find an enemy in the compound, we shoot to kill. Ok set your watches gentlemen, I make it five o'clock we move out in ten minutes. Are we all clear on that?*'

'Yep, nobody's allowed in the compound without your permission,' Derek said.

Hearing Derek's voice brought me back to the present.

'Good, right I'm off. See you later,' Sherwood said as he left the gatehouse.

'Yeah, see you later, you prick,' I said

'Watch it Mickey, he nearly heard you.'

'So what? The blokes a prick, he's full of crap.'

I really didn't like the arsehole, there was something about him that really pissed me off, but I'd put up with bigger twats than him on a daily basis in the army.

Dave Sherwood had been in the army too. I'd heard he'd worked in the stores, in other words he was a blanket stacker, but what pissed me off was he told everyone he was a paratrooper. What a load of bollocks.

'Are you still seeing your bit of stuff down London? What was her name, Chrissie?' Derek asked glancing at me.

I didn't answer him. I wasn't in the mood to talk about my private life.

'I don't know how you do it. How is Debbie and the kids?'

'What's this? *Have ago at Mickey week?* for fucks sake.'

A few months ago me and Derek met up downtown for a few beers. I made the mistake of telling Derek my life story, we've all done it. That night I got a load of shit off my chest, he obviously remembered everything I said. All he does now, is bring up all my gremlins, when he's got nothing else to talk about.

'Me and Deb's aren't together anymore and they're not my kids. It might have escaped your notice they're a different colour to me. I'll put that down to you getting on a bit, you blind twat.'

I met Debbie nine years ago, she was my first serious girlfriend. We split up two years later, she couldn't handle me being away all the time.

She married CJ soon after we split up, they had two kids together, then she divorced him after four years, on the grounds of domestic violence. When I found out CJ had been knocking Debbie about, I wanted to make him pay, but I backed off on Debbie's orders. It was a chapter in her life she wanted to put behind her. CJ wasn't allowed within two miles of the property, but she knew that wouldn't stop him. That's why she always kept a baseball bat beside the bed at night, in case he came back. She was right, he did ignore the restraining order.

A few months later, while she was out picking up the kids from nursery, he climbed in through the bathroom window and then hid in the loft. Later that night as she was lying in bed half asleep, she heard a noise, it was CJ climbing down from the loft, but she heard him and was ready for him. As soon as he dropped onto the landing, she swung the baseball bat as hard as she could at him. The force of the blow knocked him off his feet and down the stairs, he was out cold. She called the police and they took him away. After that, he spent a few weeks in prison and lost all visiting rights to the kids, she hadn't seen him since.

Suddenly she was single again with two kids, and living in a house where she couldn't make the mortgage payments. The house was in her name, her dad gave her the deposit before he died, she was weeks away from losing the house. That's when I appeared back on the scene. I was on extended leave due to my injuries. We soon got back together. I managed to get enough money together to keep the mortgage company happy for a while.

Then I got made redundant, and with the redundancy money I paid off her arrears and gave her a lump sum to re-mortgage the house, so her monthly payments were lower and affordable, if ever I moved on. Debbie didn't ask me to pay, I just did it. That was two years ago.

I moved in and for the first few months we were really happy, but things began to change. We could never rekindle the relationship we had nine years earlier, there was too much water under the bridge. For the last six months, our relationship had been strained, we both still had feelings for each other, but the romance had gone a long time ago.

'Right, I'm off,' Derek said handing me back my newspaper, 'have a good day mate and I'll see you Monday night.'

'Give my regards to the missus and your son.'

ɪ do,' he said as he left the gatehouse.

## CHAPTER 3

In another ten minutes it would start to get busy. From seven to nine, I had to man the gatehouse, lift the barriers and check ID's, which basically meant sucking up to staff and taking abuse from the cheeky students.

I remember my interview for the job, one of the questions was 'Do you think you can handle the students? They can be a handful at times.'

I thought, *are you fucking real or what?* Instead I bit my lip and smiled and said 'no problem.'

I'd taken the job centre's advice by then and rewritten my CV. I just had time to drink the cup of tea I'd made, and send Chrissie a text. *"Hi Sexy, flying back today, can't wait to see you, arriving on the 15.34 train tomorrow. Xxx"*

Chrissie was modelling for fashion catalogues and had expensive tastes. I couldn't believe my luck when she fell for me that night. She was slightly taller than me, blond, blue eyed, with curves in all the right places.

I was stationed in Colchester at the time. Myself and a few of my army mates decided to head to London for the weekend, on a bender, after a six, month tour to Afghanistan.

We thought it would be a good idea and a bit of a laugh to get suited up and pose as special agents to fool the ladies, a bit of a James Bond thing. We were all loaded with cash after the tour. It worked a treat. The three girls we met that night fell for it, and they were stunning.

The good thing about that scam was if any of the girls asked us what we did for a living, we couldn't tell them. Well, it was all about, the official secrets act, wasn't it? We could be MI5, SAS or any other agency.

That was five years ago, the other two lads didn't go back for more, but I did, her name was Chrissie. I really liked her. She never asked me any questions about what I was all about, at the same time I didn't ask her about what she did, all I knew was she worked in the fashion industry. I just turned up every now and again. As long as I had a full wallet and I could keep up with her expensive tastes, she seemed happy.

At first that wasn't a problem, I had a good salary and no financial obligations. I should have ended things with her when I moved in with Debbie, but I loved them both, for different reasons. After being de-mobbed I had a bank account full of redundancy money, but after helping Debbie out and spending thousands on my flash bit of stuff, my money had nearly run out. To keep up the pretence I needed more money and fast. In a few months, I'd be screwed, the money would run out and Chrissie would be off the radar.

I thought about asking Debbie to re-mortgage the house, but I couldn't do that. I could forget about Chrissie, but that wasn't an option either, I loved everything about her. She was my type, she understood me, even though most of the stuff that came out of my mouth was bullshit, and most of all the sex was out of this world. I knew I'd have to think of something to bring more money in. One thing I was good at was problem solving, but I was running out of time.

# The Goat Killer

The first to arrive on site were the cleaners to sign for the keys. There were eight of them altogether, all different characters, all with their own problems. I was a good listener, but wished I wasn't sometimes. Then a face appeared I'd never seen before, he approached me and introduced himself.

'Hi mate, you must be Mick. Sam Spacey,' he put his hand out expecting me to shake it. 'I'm the new security guard. They told me at control that you'll be training me up.'

I just looked at him like he was a piece of shit. I don't know why, but I took an instant dislike to him.

'Did they… you can tell them at control they're a bunch of cunts.'

I don't know what it is, but most of the security guards I've met since I've been here are complete pricks. Once you get talking to them, all they talk about is... I've done this, I've done that, been everywhere, done everything stories. It's all bullshit. It's as they feel they have to impress you to excuse their shitty life.

I always feel like saying 'of course you are pal, that's why you're a fucking security guard like me. Deal with it, just be who you are.'

He just stood there like a spare prick at a wedding. If he thought he'd get a warm welcome from me, he was wrong.

'Is there somewhere I can dump my gear?' he asked.

I couldn't be arsed to answer him. I was pissed off. Why did they keep sending me these people to train up? I just don't need the aggravation.

'So, how come they've sent you here? Oh, I get it, you're Derek's replacement, God help us. Grab yourself a quick brew before the mad rush starts,' I said, realising I'd have to speak to him sooner or later.

'Cheers Mick.'

'My name is Mickey by the way... Right, job spec. Only let people in if they have ID's. You'll find the assignment instructions on the shelf, everything you need to know is in there, that's it your fully trained. Any questions?'

'What if they've forgotten their ID or lost it?'

The cleaners couldn't help but eavesdrop on the conversation. I could see them straining to hear what was being said. They seemed to know all the gossip, doing the rounds of the college, the nosey sods.

'Good question. We take them into the wood over to your left, where you'll find a small green wooden hut, tie them to the chair then, beat the living shit out of them. After that we start taking their teeth out one by one.'

Sam looked shocked, for a moment I thought he'd believed me. Obviously this dick head had no sense of humour.

'Take no notice of him. He's having you on,' Beryl the cleaning supervisor said. 'All you do, love, if they haven't got an ID, is direct them to human resources near reception, and they'll issue them with temporary ID.'

I let him do the first half hour while I read the paper, purposely missing out the double page spread on my old regiment marching through the town. I remember the last time I took part in one of those marches, I hated it. Yes, you had the people that stopped and cheered, but everyone knew most people in town that day couldn't' give a flying fuck.

## The Goat Killer

I know for a fact a lot of the people never had a clue why we were over in Afghanistan. All they saw were soldiers coming home, either injured or in a coffin, deep down I'm sure they couldn't give a shit. I didn't let it bother me that much. But what really pissed me off was groups of radical lefties with their death to British soldiers, placards. I wish our SA80's, were loaded that day, I would have had no problem emptying a magazine of twenty on them, and I wouldn't be on my own, fucking scumbags. I can remember as we marched past them, one of our lads shouted 'Fix Bayonet's!' We all burst out laughing, but the soldier got extra duties.

Just then I could hear some commotion outside, I walked out to see what it was all about. I arrived at the barrier to see a familiar face.

'You again?' I said. My voice came out sharper than I had expected.

'He hasn't got an ID,' Sam replied. It seemed he was taking the job seriously.

'It's ok, I'll deal with it.'

I turned to speak to the person who was causing the commotion.

'You're suspended remember? I suggest you turn round and get your arse off campus.'

'I've got a meeting with the vice principal and my mentor at nine.'

Simon Ashford, Ash to his mates, stood there with a smirk on his face. Little did I know at that time, this guy would end up being a big part of my life.

Ash by name, Ash by nature, he was also the campus drug dealer and a pain in the fucking arse. A right cheeky little shit. Three days ago I'd taken a handful of cannabis seeds off him, the reason for his current suspension.

He was nearly eighteen and this was his second year as a horticulture student, but even though he was a bright student, his attendance record was shocking.

I think this was judgment day for Ash, he'd already had a written warning for fighting, if it was up to me I'd kick him off campus in a heartbeat.

'Wait there, while I make some checks to make sure you're not bullshitting me.'

'Oh yeah... When do I get my property back?' he asked, pausing to spit on the road.

'What property?' I played dumb.

'My seeds, if you don't give me them back, I'll have you done for theft.'

He carried on being cheeky while I was on the phone. Yes, he was telling the truth, he'd got a meeting.

'Your meeting is at nine o'clock in the main hall, and guess what? I've got to be there,' I said, grinning from ear to ear.

'Why, what for?'

'So when they kick you off your course, I can take great pleasure in kicking your arse all the way down the driveway, and off campus.'

I was by now inches away from his ugly face. The urge to punch him was overwhelming.

'Fuck you. You can't talk to me like that, I could get you suspended and your breath smells. What did you eat for breakfast, pig shit?'

He started to stress me out. The next minute I imagined myself pushing him to the ground, placing my foot violently across his scrawny neck, and raising my rifle above my head and bringing it down bayonet fixed. Then listening to the sickening sound of the blade penetrating his empty skull.

'I want to go to the canteen first, for a coffee.'

Ash's voice brought me to my senses. The day dreams were getting worse. I was just glad I hadn't followed through with the actions I'd dreamed about.

'Yes ok, but you're not going alone. Sam, can you go with him? Don't let him wander out of your sight.'

I sat down and gathered my thoughts. Ever since the incident, these violent day dreams always came to me when I got stressed out. The trouble was they seemed so real.

'You ok Mickey?' Beryl asked. On her face, I could read her concern for me.

'Yes, I'm fine, don't you worry.' A trickle of sweat ran down my back.

The rest of the day went by quickly. Ash got a stay of execution, but one more fuck up and he was gone. I felt sorry for him, he reminded me of myself when I was his age. He would be the sort of lad that would do well in the forces, once he was knocked into shape.

I got home around half six that evening. I found a note on the table from Debbie, telling me she'd gone to her mum's in Nottingham for a few days. I didn't believe that for one minute, I was sure she had someone else. I wasn't bothered though, as long as it wasn't her ex, but I knew she wasn't that stupid.

I thought I'd have an early night, I'd get up early and head down to London for a few days, to see Chrissie. After all, this would be my last visit for a while, until I'd sorted out some cash. I really needed to think of a way to get more money, funds were running low.

I lay in bed thinking what to say to her, about why I wouldn't be back down for a while. I decided I'd just spin another ask no questions' story, it pissed her off a bit, but she knew I was just doing what I do.

I felt things had got a bit more serious between us lately. I didn't think telling her I was an ordinary bloke, who lived with my ex- girlfriend and her two kids trying to survive on just above the minimum wage, would go down well. But, I also knew it wouldn't be long, before she let me know she wanted more than a long distance relationship.

# CHAPTER 4

I slept well that night for the first time in a while, no bad dreams. I showered, packed my grip and headed for the station, leaving Debbie a note that I would be back tomorrow evening. Debbie didn't mind me pissing off for a day or two, as long as she knew when I was coming back. If I didn't let her know, she'd worry about me.

It was a two, hour train journey down to London, a journey I'd made loads of times. The carriage I was in was almost empty, apart from a few late commuters tapping away on their laptops and tablets. I gazed out of the window, it wasn't long before I was in deep thought. How the fuck can I make some serious money? Should I come clean with Chrissie? No, she'd definitely tell me to sling my hook. I'd have to tell her one day, if I ever wanted to settle down with her. I laughed to myself, me, settling down, my mates would find that thought hilarious.

Then my thoughts turned back to money, I took my wallet out to see how much I'd got on me. One hundred and fifteen quid and a pocket full of cannabis seeds, that's all I had. It wasn't enough; pay day wasn't for another week.

How much are cannabis seeds worth, I thought. I looked over at a young mother reading a story to her son, he must have been around three. The title of the book was *Jack and the beanstalk*, that was a funny coincidence. There's me sitting with a bag full of cannabis seeds, and this mother was telling her son how Jack had planted the beans in the garden, and we all know what happened after that.

I sat deep in thought for a few minutes, and then it came to me. That's it, I'd got it, I had my money making idea. It was perfect, a bit crazy, but it just might work. For the rest of the journey, the more I thought about it, the more it made sense. I couldn't think of anything else for the remainder of the ride.

I arrived at St Pancras station. As always when she could, Chrissie was there to meet me. She ran towards me like she always did, and wrapped her arms around me and gave me the biggest hug. Our meetings always reminded me of one of those old fashioned, black and white, smoky station, movie scenes. It was always the same, even if the platform was packed with commuters, she didn't care.

'God I've missed you, Mickey. I've got so much to tell you.'

We made our way to the underground, to get on the Northern line to Golders Green, where she rented a flat. She didn't shut up talking until we opened her flat door.

'I bet you're tired, aren't you, and all I've been doing is talk. Why don't you take a relaxing shower, while I make you a nice cup of coffee?'

'Sounds like a plan,' I said as I entered the bedroom.

The bedroom was always immaculate, everything was clean, her favourite colour was lilac, which was obvious from the amount of lilac things in the room. I stripped off and jumped in the shower. She had already put out my shower gel, razor, shaving foam and a towel. She was always one step ahead, that's what I liked about her.

# The Goat Killer

I'd been in the shower five minutes, when I had the feeling I was being watched. I turned around and she just stood there staring at me. How long had she been standing there? I started to wash my privates.

'Here, let me do that for you,' she said with a smile.

Chrissie walked over and took hold of me with both hands, her grip was very firm. Smiling, she glanced down at my now fully erect penis.

'Do you like me doing that?' She looked straight into my eyes.

'Yes, he's missed you.'

'I can tell. We'll save him for later, shall we?'

'You are one teasing bitch,' I said. My body felt like it was on fire.

She squeezed my penis hard, it took me by surprise, as I wasn't expecting it.

'I can be a bitch if you want me to be.' She turned her back and walked off.

I finished showering and put my clothes back on. She began telling me what we were doing that evening. I was hoping we'd stay in, watch a movie, have a few bottles of wine and fuck, but as always Chrissie had other ideas. Hearing what her plans were, my thoughts turned to my financial situation and the pittance I had in my wallet.

'Chrissie...I've got a bit of a problem. I didn't bring much money with me.'

'Don't worry about it, it's sorted. Tonight is a freebie, Giles is paying. We're going Greek.'

'Who's Giles?' The name didn't ring a bell.

'Giles is a very, good friend of mine. I'm sure I've mentioned him to you before.'

'Oh, *that Giles*, the guy you work for?'

'Yes, my boss, he owns Retro Fashions.'

In all the time I'd known Chrissie, she'd only mentioned him once. The only thing I remember her telling me was that she thought he was a little creepy, and now we were going out for a meal with him. Great, this should be interesting.

It was seven o'clock when we made our way downstairs and jumped in a taxi. Chrissie gave the driver directions and we headed for The Vine, a Greek restaurant, Giles was already there. He saw us getting out of the cab, and headed for the door to greet us. The word beanpole, sprang to mind on my first sight of him. Tall and skinny, wearing a designer suit and handmade shoes, his wealth was obvious.

'Hi Giles, this is Mickey,' Chrissie said. Her voice had a happy note.

'Nice to meet you at last Mickey.' We shook hands politely. I hoped this would be our first and last meeting. The guy was so obviously a knob.

We sat down and ordered drinks, I had a beer, while Chrissie had her usual dry white wine. Giles was drinking gin and orange. While the drinks were on the way, I scanned the menu. I was starving, I hadn't eaten all day, apart from an over-priced, sweaty cheese sandwich, from the train buffet car. We all ordered our food and Giles started a conversation going.

'So we meet at last, *the famous Mickey*, according to Chrissie here.'

As he said that, Giles placed his hand on Chrissie's. I didn't like that. My first thought was he better be gay, he must be gay, Chrissie wouldn't cheat on me, would she?

'That's all she talks about, Mickey this, Mickey that. I understand you work for the government.'

'Sort of...'

'So, what sort of work do you do Mickey?'

Chrissie interrupted, 'you're wasting your time Giles. Mickey won't tell you anything, or should I say he can't tell you anything.'

'Oh come on, you can tell us something. Surely your job can't be that important, can it?'

I thought it best not to answer him. I didn't like the bloke, but he was a friend of Chrissie's, so I had to be on my best behaviour.

'Ok, I understand. I was in the army you know.'

'Really? What mob were you in?' It was obvious he had been an officer. He wouldn't have lasted five minutes in the ranks.

Giles smiled and started to giggle, like a naughty schoolboy.

'I can't tell you that. You see, I can have my secrets as well you know.'

Chrissie laughed, she found it funny, I didn't, I'd set myself up for that one, hadn't I. Giles was starting to piss me off. The guy was a fucking arsehole. He was trying to belittle me. I was getting stressed out big time. The starter arrived and I breathed a sigh of relief, hopefully he'd be too busy eating to carry on talking.

We all started to eat but, after a few mouthfuls, Giles started talking shite again. I think he'd had too much to drink. I'd watched him down four drinks before the food arrived. Suddenly Giles stood up and excused himself, and headed for the toilets. I watched him until he disappeared from sight. If Chrissie was hoping I'd become friends with him, she was going to be disappointed.

'What's the matter babe?' Chrissie asked.

'Your Giles is a prick.'

'Oh don't say that. Giles is just Giles, give him a chance, he's just had a bit too much to drink.'

'What is he to you anyway?'

'I told you he's my boss, and he owns the flat I live in.'

'Are you fucking him?'

Chrissie dropped her knife and fork. If looks could kill, I'd be dead.

'I'm not even going to dignify that with an answer.'

There were a few minutes, silence, as we sat staring at each other, then I apologised.

'I'm sorry Chrissie, I don't know why I said that. I've just had a very stressful week at work. I'd love to answer all his questions, but I can't. I came here to see you, not to be interrogated by him.'

Chrissie leaned over and kissed me on the cheek. That's the kind of person she was, forgiving.

'It's ok babe, I know your job must be stressful and I love a jealous man,' and then she raised her voice, 'and the only person fucking me is you.'

The people around us turned their heads towards us, some smiled, some were disgusted. At that moment, my stress levels just disappeared, she was the only person who could do that.

I stood up and headed for the toilets. I walked in, to find Giles snorting a large amount of cocaine. I started to have a piss, trying to ignore him. If he wanted to scramble his brain, it was none of my business.

'Want some?' Giles offered.

'No thanks, I don't use that shit.'

'Royal Engineers.'

'What?'

'I was in the Royal Engineers, only for a few years. I was an officer, a second lieutenant, I hated it.'

My gut feeling was right. I can smell them from miles away.

'I did it for my father, he was a major in the Engineers for twenty-two years. He went straight up through the ranks from private to Major. I would still be in now if he were alive. He dropped dead two years after I joined and left me the family estate.'

'That was good of him.'

'The man was an arse. I knew if I didn't join up, he'd leave me nothing.'

I finished pissing and started washing my hands. He stood beside the wash basin.

'Look, sorry if I was a bit off with you out there, in front of Chrissie.'

'That's ok. If you weren't Chrissie's friend, I'd have ripped your fucking head off,' I said, walking towards the door. I knew if I didn't leave, I'd end up punching his lights out.

We both arrived back at our table. The rest of the evening went well, but there was still an atmosphere between me and Giles. We finished our meal and three bottles of wine, mostly drunk by him. It was time to leave. The bill arrived on the table and he picked it up.

'It's ok, my treat.'

We said our goodbyes, leaving Giles to pay the bill.

From the moment we climbed in the taxi, we couldn't keep our hands off each other. We arrived back at the flat, the sex was good, but because of the booze it didn't last long, usually we'd be at it all night.

I woke up during the night and glanced over at the alarm clock, it was four in the morning, Chrissie was fast asleep. I'd woken up from one of my many bad dreams. I got out of bed and sat down in the living room in the dark, and lit up a cigarette. This time I couldn't remember what the dream was about. It wasn't long before my thoughts drifted to my money making plan. If it worked, it would solve all my problems, and get me to where I really wanted to be.

'What's up, can't you sleep? Come back to bed, babe. What are you thinking about?'

'Oh, nothing important.'

Chrissie walked up behind me, leaned over the back of the sofa and put her arms around me.

'What's troubling you, babe? My Mickey, the mystery man. Do you have to go back? Can't you stay for a few more days, or even better forever would be good.'

'I'd love to sweetheart, but you know how it is.'

Before I could say another word, she just put a finger to her lips and told me to shush. She sat down on the sofa and cuddled up next to me.

'When are you going to be mine Mickey Saunders?'

I didn't answer her, I finished off my cigarette, picked Chrissie up in my arms, carried her back to the bedroom, and laid her back on the bed. We both fell into an exhausted sleep in minutes.

The next thing I heard was the busy rush hour traffic, which alerted me to the fact I should be up, getting ready to leave. I'd planned to catch the five to eleven train back to Derby. I leaned over to put my arms round Chrissie, but she wasn't there, I was on my own in the bed. I put on my dressing gown and walked to the kitchen, to find a full English breakfast, tomatoes, mushrooms and a perfect fried egg and bacon waiting for me.

'Was it the smell of the bacon that woke you up?'

'It must have been. You spoil me.'

Chrissie stood in the middle of the kitchen wearing just her knickers. She looked so inviting, but I didn't have time for that now. I began to eat my breakfast.

'Where's yours?' On the table there was only my plate.

'Are you kidding? I can't touch that lot, I'm a model. Just toast and black coffee for me.'

I finished my breakfast, then showered and got myself ready.

'When will I be seeing you again mystery man?'

'I'll text you.'

'You always say that.'

We hugged and said our goodbyes in the flat. I walked up the busy street, glad to be on my way home. Even though I loved being with Chrissie, I was always a little relieved to leave. Chrissie tended to get clingier and clingier the longer I stopped. Looking back up at the flat window, there she was, waving away and blowing me the odd kiss. I felt a bit guilty, but I got what I wanted and so did she, I suppose. We drank, we feasted, we fucked, and now less than twenty- four hours later, I was on my way back to Derby.

## CHAPTER 5

It was now time to concentrate on my money making idea. I had a mission, a plan, and it was a good one, a bit crazy, but if it worked it would make me a lot of money, and solve a multitude of problems.

Arriving back in Derby, I decided to check in with my brother. I sat down and told him my money making plan in fine detail. It felt like we were back in the army, barking orders before a mission.

'So, what do you reckon?' I was on tenterhooks waiting for his reply. He was my big brother and I wanted his approval. I didn't stop long, I never did. I did the usual and left him a few beers.

'See you later, bro. You take care, see you again soon.'

Ten minutes later I arrived home. Debbie was sitting in the kitchen reading one of her girlie mags or training manuals, as I like to call them. The ones that are full of 'Men are all bastards' stories. They were just as likely to get her in the mood to moan at me.

'You're back then? Have a good trip did you, where ever you went.'

'How's your mum?' I asked.

'She's fine, why do you ask?'

'I thought she was in Skegness this week, on holiday.'

She didn't answer my question, but came back with an equally awkward question, it was like a chess match.

'So where you been?'

'Nowhere important. I just went to see a few of my ex-army mates, that's all.'

To be honest, I couldn't give a flying fuck where she'd been or who with, as long as it was someone that cared for her. I think I know who she's seeing and if I'm right, she'll be treated like a queen.

I still loved her, but it was more like I was her big brother, with the occasional shag thrown in when she was feeling horny. I decided to up the stakes and play a little game.

'I was round Daz's, that's where I was.'

That put her on the spot. Her body language gave her away, it was official, Debbie was shagging my best mate Daz. She couldn't question me about it, because that was where she had been, check mate.

'How is he?' Her faked disinterest gave her away.

'He's fine. He was telling me he was a bit frustrated. He hasn't had a decent shag for months.' I was enjoying my little game. 'I suppose having no legs doesn't help, I bet it's a bit of a turn off for most women.'

'That's a horrible thing to say. What's having no legs got to do with it?' she asked in a gentle voice.

'Chill out, Daz wouldn't give a shit. Us, ex squaddies, have got the sickest, darkest, sense of humour.'

It was game over, Debbie was definitely shagging Daz.

'You can keep your sick sense of humour to yourself. I don't want to hear it.'

I couldn't be arsed with making something to eat, so I popped out for some fast food to eat later. We sat watching Big Brother, filling our faces with burger and chips. It was letters day on Big Brother, it was a few days before they announced the winner, and they got to read to each other their letters from home.

What a load of shite, they've only been apart a few fucking weeks and there they are bawling their fucking eyes out, 'pathetic,' are the rest of the country really like this? I muted the TV to Debbie's annoyance.

'Oi, I'm watching that.'

'I can remember the last letter you sent me Debbie, I still have it. The Dear John letter. I kept all your letters.'

'Shut up Mickey, don't remind me.'

'I'll go and get it if you want.'

'You haven't still got it, have you? Really.' She looked at me as if I was pulling her leg.

I returned from the bedroom with the letter, and started to read. Debbie hid her face in shame, by burying it in one of the cushions. She made a lunge and tried to grab the letter, but I was too quick for her.

*'My Dearest Darling Mickey,*
*I don't know how to tell you this. I might as well get straight to the point. I'm sorry Mickey, but I don't think there is any point in us staying together. I wanted to tell you this before you left to go back, but I didn't want to upset you.*
*You love the army and I have to respect that. That is the career path you've chosen, but I can't handle it, sitting here waiting for you to come home, that's if you come home.*
*I don't think I could deal with it if something happened to you, so I think the best thing I could do is be honest and up front with you, I want us to split up. I'm sorry to break this news to you while you're out there, but I wanted to be truthful to you, it's the least you deserve.*
*I'm really, really sorry*
*Debbie*
*Xxx'*

I folded the letter, Debbie was looking at her nails, I could see she was upset. Perhaps it hadn't been a good idea to read that letter. It was too late anyway.

'Six months later you were married to that wanker and you'd had a kid. How the fuck did that happen Debbie? Being dumped was bad enough, but why didn't you tell me you were up the duff with somebody else's kid, and how did you know it was his? I was shagging you at the time, I must have been.' The feeling of betrayal still hurt, even now.

'I knew it wasn't yours.'

'How?'

'Because I did.'

'It's pretty obvious now he's not mine.'

'I'm sorry, Mickey.'

'All water under the bridge now. It's ok, shit happens, you were young.' I tried to be sympathetic, but I couldn't.

'You broke my fucking heart Deb.' I said, looking directly at her.

'What did you do, how did you take it?' she asked as tears filled her eyes.

'How do you fucking think I took it? I was gutted.'

'Did you cry?'

'No, I strangled a goat.'

'What?' Debbie looked at me in disbelief.

'I remember finishing reading the letter. All I wanted to do was take my anger out on something or someone. Unfortunately, there happened to be a goat that wouldn't stop bleating, so I strangled it. The owner wasn't too happy. He had just spent the last half hour trying to sell it to me.'

'Oh the poor thing.'

'Fuck the goat, what about poor me... I remember the locals went crazy, we had to pay them off.'

'So you killed a goat because I dumped you.'
'Yes, but don't worry, the troops all had goat stew that night.'
'That's so sad.'
What started off as a bit of an awkward evening, turned into an enjoyable one. That's what life was like between us. Yes, we both had lovers, both had fucked up lives, but we both knew that one would always look out for the other, soul mates forever.

I got up the next morning for work at five o'clock as usual, this time no bad dreams. I left Debbie in bed, there was no school for the kids today. I washed and put on my nice clean uniform. I'll say one thing for Debbie, there was always a pressed shirt in the wardrobe. I grabbed my pack up and headed for work. For once I was feeling positive, today was the day to put my plan into action. I'd seen Chrissie, Debbie was in a good mood, and everything was going to be ok, I could feel it. I did my usual and picked up my paper and tobacco.

'Morning Naz.'
'Morning, Mickey, here's your paper and baccy.'
'Cheers, what's this, no cricket?' I asked, noticing the TV was turned off.
'No, not this morning, very busy, I'm stock taking.'
'Ok, I won't stay for a chat then, see you tomorrow.'

## CHAPTER 6

I arrived at work to find Derek not there. I was relieving Sam. The guy I'd trained up a few days ago.

'Where's Derek?' I asked, Sam's presence put me in a bad mood.

'Apparently he phoned in sick. They asked me to stand in for him. They said they tried to get in touch with you, to ask if you'd do it.' Sam said.

'They haven't got a hope in hell, I do enough hours for this company. Oh well, I hope he's ok, the old fucker, one in a million our Derek.'

'They asked me to cover Derek's shift until further notice. I hate working nights.'

'I'll tell you what, I'll do your nights if you want, you can do my days.' Nothing could have been better. That was one problem solved.

'Would you do that?'

'I've just fucking said I would haven't I? You get off home, I'll have words with control. We'll start at the weekend if they agree to it.'

Quick thinking on my part. Being on regular nights would help me in what I was about to do.

'I'll leave it with you thanks. I'll see you in the week.' Sam said, grabbing his jacket and walking off down the driveway.

The cleaners arrived to sign for their keys, I just handed them out automatically, my thoughts were on my plan. Now I had one thing on my mind, Ash. He would be walking up the drive shortly, and was about to find out he was going to be a major part of my plan. I might have known he would be the last student to arrive on site, late as usual.

'You're late.' I said, as Ash approached the gatehouse.

'I.D please.' I requested.

'For fuck's sake, as though you don't know who I am by now.' He replied, trying to brush past me.

'You're late.'

'No, I'm not. My first lesson doesn't start until ten o'clock.'

'So what are you going to be doing until then?'

'What's it to do with you?'

I began to wonder if I could work with the little shit. Why did he have to be so fucking annoying?

'I need to talk to you.'

'What about?' he asked, frowning.

'It's about you getting your cannabis seeds back, and other stuff. Come and see me at five o'clock.'

'What if I don't?'

'Come with me, I want to show you something.' I said, guiding him towards the gatehouse.

'Fuck off, are you some kind of perv?'

Ash entered the gatehouse reluctantly. I could tell he was nervous.

'Watch this.'

I pressed play on the CCTV system. Ash sat there watching himself in the canteen

'Look, it's you on my TV, 11.54 Wednesday the 16$^{th}$ that is you isn't it?'

The scene on the CCTV showed him clearly selling drugs to other students. Ash folded his arms, sat back, and stared out of the window, acting as though he wasn't bothered.

'You're fucked mate, course over, and I'm sure the police would be interested in seeing this.'

'So what now?'

I pulled my hand out of my pocket, and handed him his seeds.

'I don't understand.'

'They're yours, aren't they? You'll understand at five o'clock. Make sure you're here, or I'll be showing that CCTV footage to the vice principal.'

Ash just left without saying a word, I didn't know if he'd come back at five o'clock. I didn't want to threaten him with the CCTV images, but it was the only way to grab his attention

The rest of the day went really slowly. I contacted control and they gave me the go ahead to switch from days to nights. I hated nights too, but it was all part of the plan. Five o'clock arrived and there was a knock on the gatehouse door.

'Come in,' I said.

The college was nearly empty, just a few staff left on site prepping for the next day. Ash sat down.

'I'll get straight to the point. I want you to teach me everything you know about growing cannabis.'

Ash started to laugh, then paused.

'Are you serious? What makes you think I know how to grow it?'

'Let's say it's a hunch.'

'And how did you come to that conclusion?'

'A bright lad like you, studying horticulture and you deal it. I bet you've got a loft full of it.'

Ash stood up, and began moving towards the gatehouse door.

'Where are you going?'

'I'm off.'

'Sit down, you fucking little shit.'

He sat back down. I stood between him and the doorway.

'Yes, I did have my own weed farm going, just a few plants that's all, but the police got wind of it. Some wanker had grassed me up, luckily I got a tip off before they arrived. And by the way, for your info, I was growing the plants for my dad.

'So he's a pot head as well.'

'My dad's disabled, he has MS, he needs it to take the pain away. He's not like the people who smoke it for fun.'

'Sorry to hear that.'

'Can I go now, or are you going to get to the point.'

I thought for a minute before answering. For my plan to succeed I needed him on board.

'So, I'm guessing you need all the weed you can get for your old man, and a bit of pocket money.'

'Yes and the reason I deal is to make a few quid, so we can eat. We hardly get fuck all on benefits since they changed everything.'

It was getting to the point where I needed to know, how much we could expect to make.

'How much money can you make selling weed?'

'That's a bit of a stupid fucking question. Sky's the limit mate. I can sell it until it grows out my arse, it's the supply that's the problem.'

'I need to show you something, follow me.'

We walked the quarter mile to the old compound, we stood outside the gates.

'This is it,' I said.

Ash looked around, and straight away he sensed what I was thinking.

'I get it. You want me to turn this place into a cannabis farm. You're having a fucking laugh aren't you? Right under the principal's nose, tell me your joking.' Ash started to laugh.

'You got it in one.'

'This is so fucked up, dude. You don't know the first thing about growing cannabis.'

'I know I don't, but you're going to teach me everything I need to know.'

'Why this place?'

'It's perfect. It's far enough away from the campus to go unnoticed, it's fenced off, it backs onto a canal, it's got a water supply and electricity and I'm the only one with the key.' I said, as I jangled the key in Ash's face.

'But won't they want to come in here from time to time?'

'What for? It's been classed as derelict. They don't want anyone, anywhere near it until next year. The college has put in for a grant so they can rebuild on it. Until then it's out of bounds. It's a health and safety risk, so the only person with access is me, because I'm the only one with a key. If any staff wanted to get access, they'd have to see me first, and I'm sure I can persuade them it would be a bad idea. Think about it, the only way to get to it is via the gatehouse. Like I said, it's fucking perfect, it backs onto the canal and if that's not enough deterrent, there's CCTV all around the place.'

'Are they working?' Ash asked, looking worried.

'They haven't been working for years, but who's to know.'

Ash started to laugh.

'What are you, laughing at you, twat?'

'It's a good plan. It's that good I want to show you something, follow me.' Ash said.

He walked to the back of the compound, to a small hole in the fence and climbed through. I followed him through, then into one the many poly tunnels. The heat inside brought beads of sweat out on my face.

'I think someone's beat you to it, Mickey.'

I was shocked to see four young, healthy cannabis plants growing happily in the corner. I couldn't believe some arsehole had got here first.

'Bastard, who the fuck put them here?'

'They're mine.' Ash said, laughing.

I looked at him in disbelief. The little shit had pulled a fast one on me.

'Why do you think I was bringing the seeds to college? I would have had this poly tunnel half full by now, that's why I was pissed off with you. These are the plants I managed to get out of my house before the police raid.'

I must admit I was impressed, the entrance he'd created was well hidden, it also meant we wouldn't have to use the main gates. This little shit was well ahead of me, and in a way I was relieved, we were sailing in the same direction. We left the compound and headed back to the gatehouse.

'So what's the deal, seeing as you want to steal my idea?' Ash said.

'Your idea? I'll give you forty percent of what we make.' The cheeky little shit. Who did he think he was talking to?

'Forget it, it's fifty, fifty or no deal.'

'Hold on a minute, I'm the one taking all the risks here.'

'What about me? It's me who'll be harvesting it and selling it no doubt. What will you be doing?'

'The same as you.' I wanted to have a piece of the action for myself.

'But you don't know the first thing about growing weed, and what about selling it, where are all your contacts? Without me, you're fucked.'

He was right. I didn't show it, but I liked the way he was talking. To be honest, I'm not greedy and the money wasn't that important to me, as long as it made enough to sort me out. I put out my hand for Ash to shake.

'Ok. Fifty, fifty it is then. I want to fill every one of them greenhouses and poly tunnels with weed plants.'

'You have no idea what's involved in doing that, do you?' Ash said.

He started to educate me on weed production, now I was the student.

'We need good quality seeds and they don't come cheap. The best seed you can get for greenhouses and poly tunnels is available via the internet. I can order it online off a Dutch site. I've used them before they're the best. Get that out on the street and they'd come running from miles around. Poor seeds always give poor weed, invest in the best you can get. Greenhouse-grown cannabis is incredibly potent when grown from good seed stock. I suggest we don't grow them directly in the ground, so we'll need plant pots, loads of them. Growing them in plant pots means we can easily move them if we have to. And most important, we need to find out whether the automated-watering system works.'

'It does.'

'Good, we're going to need it.'

'So how many more seeds will you need, and how much will they cost?' I wanted to know every last detail of the business.

'We'll need a few hundred, the going rate is around twenty-five pounds for ten.'

'Around five hundred pounds then. I'll have the money for you by the weekend. What else do you need?'

'Nothing, just the money for now.'

## CHAPTER 7

Time had gone by quickly, it was six in the evening and my relief had arrived. I arranged to meet Ash the next day after work, at his local pub, the Anchor. I arrived home to find some guy knocking on the front door forcefully.

'Can I help you mate, who are you?'

'I need to speak to Missus Debbie Morris.'

'What about? She's obviously not in.'

'She is in, sir. I saw her arrive back from picking up her kids at half four. Are you related to her?'

'I'll ask you again, who the fuck, are you?'

I started to get angry and moved in front of him. He went to get something out of his pocket. I was on him like a rash. The next moment I was back in Afghanistan. I pushed him against the wall, put him in a headlock and started searching him for weapons.

'What the hell are you doing, are you mad?'

He could be friendly or he could be Taliban, you couldn't trust no one out here. I decided to take him down on the ground until backup arrived, but there was no backup, just Debbie and the two kids looking down at me open mouthed.

'What the hell are you doing?'

'It's ok Debbie, he's clear.'

I pulled the guy up and dusted him off. All the while, Debbie was giving me a look that said, *you fucking idiot*.

'Sorry pal, but you can never be too careful nowadays,' I said, as a parting shot.

## The Goat Killer

I brushed past Debbie and went into the house. I headed for the kitchen, went to the sink and poured myself a glass of water. I could hear Debbie outside apologising.

'I'm really... Really sorry, Mister Gamble, it won't happen again.'

'It better not. Who is he, what's up with him?'

I heard her whispering, although her whisper was like someone talking through a megaphone. I heard every word she said, 'It's ok, he served in Afghanistan, he's a bit stressed.'

'I don't care where he's been, there was no need for that. Does he know who I am?'

'Again, I'm really sorry. Here's your money,' Debbie said handing over a white envelope, 'there's two weeks' worth there, I won't be here next week, I'll be at my mum's.'

'He really needs to see someone, before he does something he'll regret.'

Fuck this, that was it, I'd heard more than enough shit from the wanker. I put my glass down and headed for the door. Just as I got there Debbie shut it and spread her arms out, preventing me from opening it.

'No Mickey. You're not going out there. I've got enough on my plate, without you starting a war with the Gamble's.'

I sat down in the living room and switched the TV on, to drown out Debbie's voice. I could hear her muttering to herself in the hallway. It wasn't long before she came into the living room.

'What the hell was all that about?'

'I didn't know who he was, he could have been anybody. I only did what any normal bloke would do.'

'Bollocks! You're not normal, far from it.'

'Who was he?' I couldn't stop myself asking.

'He's from easy loan.'

'Fucking hell Deb, what have I told you about loan sharks.'

Debbie disappeared into the kitchen and came back with two mugs of coffee and sat down next to me.

'Do you reckon he'll lend me some money?'

Debbie laughed, 'what, after what you've just done to him.'

'They're used to it, them lot. Bloody loan sharks, it happens to them every day.'

'What, being mistaken for Taliban suicide bombers?'

'Shut up, Debbie.'

'No I bloody won't. Do you know who he works for?'

'I couldn't give a flying fuck who he works for.'

'You should do, it's Tommy Gamble, also known as AK.'

'Never heard of him.' Was she expecting me to start quaking in my boots?

'You don't want to. No one messes with the Gamble family.'

'Whatever.'

'Why do you need money? How much do you need? I've got twenty quid in my purse if you want it.'

'I need more than that.'

'How much more?'

'A few hundred...' I spoke quietly, embarrassed at having to ask Debbie for money.

'I haven't got that sort of money. Where's all your redundancy money gone?'

'It's gone.'

Debbie knew she couldn't delve any further, after all, I'd paid most of her mortgage off, with a big percentage of my redundancy money. She left the room and came back a few minutes later.

'You can have these, they must be worth a few hundred quid,' she said, placing two rings down on the table, her wedding ring and an engagement ring. The engagement ring looked like it might be worth something. It was a platinum band with a cushion cut sapphire surrounded by tiny diamonds.

'I can't take them. They're yours.'

'I don't want them. They just bring back bad memories.'

Debbie was having none of it, and knowing her, she wouldn't back down, so I took them.

Like she said, the rings were from her failed marriage to that arsehole of a woman-beater.

It was funny to think CJ's money that paid for the rings, would be bankrolling me to buy the cannabis seeds.

'Thanks Debs, I'll pay you back a hundred times over, you'll see.'

'I don't want anything back. You've given me enough.'

She said, kissing me on the cheek.

I woke the next morning to Debbie crying, I knew what that meant, I'd been dreaming again. Her nose was bleeding. She told me I'd lashed out in my sleep, I had no memory of it. All I could do was say sorry, she said she was ok. I decided from now on I'd sleep on the downstairs sofa. Maybe it was time to visit the doctor. I got out of bed and dressed quickly, before heading downstairs. After a cup of tea, I left the house. Today would be a busy day.

First on the list were the pawnbrokers. He said the rings were worth four hundred and ninety pounds. The shark offered me two hundred and ninety for them. I had ninety days to buy them back, plus interest. It wasn't enough money, I needed more.

I spent the rest of the day on the internet. First of all, I checked my Facebook account. I'd set it up in my brother's name, he didn't mind. I hadn't been on for a while and I wanted to check what was happening in the world.

Most of my serving and ex- army mates were on there. It was on Facebook I found the sad news that my work colleague Derek, had passed away. He managed to see his new grandson in Birmingham, but when he arrived back in Derby, he suffered a massive heart attack. I was gutted, the guy had worked fucking hard all his life. He'd been looking forward to retirement and then bang, he was gone. The funeral was in three weeks, time. I made a note of the time and date, I would be going to pay my respects. I had a moment to myself thinking of the laughs we'd had, mainly taking the piss out of life. RIP Derek.

I came off Facebook and began to surf the net. I wanted to find out everything I could about cannabis and how to grow it. There was so much to take in, I never knew growing weed was so complicated.

There were so many street names for the drug depending where you came from around the country or world, there was Bhang, black, blast, blow, blunts, Bob Hope, bush, dope, draw, ganja, grass, hash, wacky baccy, weed, to name but a few. Some names were based on where it came from. The cannabis industry was massive. I read an article that said, according to the Serious and Organized Crime Agency, around two hundred and seventy tons of cannabis is consumed every year in Britain, and around eighty percent of it is grown here. I wanted a share of it. I sensed someone standing behind me, I glanced over my shoulder and Debbie was standing there.

'Why are you reading up on cannabis? You've been at it all afternoon.'

'Don't worry, it's for work. As a security guard, I need to know all about it, especially working at the college, it's everywhere.'

'If it's everywhere get me some.'
'You don't smoke that shit, do you?' I looked at her in disbelief. It was a shock to discover there were still parts of her life I knew nothing about.
'I can't afford it. CJ smoked weed all the time. He was always in the garden shed with his bong. It was when he couldn't get hold of any that he took it out on me and the kids.'
'Bastard. I'd love five minutes with him all to myself.'
I glanced at my watch, and was shocked to see how late it was.
'Shit, I need to be somewhere.'
'Where?' Debbie asked, looking straight at me.
'The Anchor. Not that it's any of your business.' I answered. Just when I need her to be her usual laid back self, she starts asking awkward questions.
'Why do you want to go to that dive? It's a wonder it hasn't been closed down, like the rest of the pubs around here. You'll be alright in there if you're after an education in drugs.'

On my way to meet Ash, I decided to give Chrissie a call. I hadn't spoken to her since my last visit, it would be nice to hear her voice.
'Hi sweetheart, how's things?'
'Ok, I suppose. Working hard as usual. We're rehearsing for a big fashion show at the weekend.'
'How's that idiot Giles?'
'He's ok, he keeps asking about you all the time. I think he likes you.'
'What sort of questions?' Why was he interested in me? Did he fancy me, was he gay?

'You know, the one I keep asking you. I told him he'd be better off keeping his nose out. We all know you can't say a word, after all it's, top secret, isn't it?'

'You can tell that knob head to mind his own fucking business.' I felt so angry. What gave him the right to pry into my life? Chrissie started laughing, which made me even angrier.

'Have you been drinking? You're pissed aren't you?'

'I might be, just a few glasses of wine after work that's all. I think I'll have an early night in my lovely soft bed, all on my own.'

'Don't be like that, I'll be coming down there soon.'

'When babe? It's ok, I know you can't tell me.'

'I'll text you ok. Are you still there?' I said, worried by the silence.

'Yes, I'm still here.'

Her last words were, "I love you, babe" and then she hung up.

Why is Giles so interested in me, I wondered? What's his problem? All kinds of thoughts started to go through my mind. Was Chrissie really jumping into an empty bed? I shook my head to try and dispel the image that began forming in my mind.

## CHAPTER 8

I walked into the Anchor and knew, instantly, Debbie was right. From the threadbare carpet to the patched seat covers, the pub had an air of neglect, it should have been shut down years ago. It left me wondering how it managed to stay open.

'Yes mate, what will it be?' Asked the fat scruffy looking guy behind the bar.

'I'll have a pint of John Smiths please. Has Ash been in today?'

'Who wants to know?'

'My name's Mickey. I'm supposed to be meeting him in here.'

'Take a seat with the rest of them. I'm sure Ash will be along shortly, that's if he's got any.'

He handed me my drink and I took a seat with my back to the wall.

I scanned around the bar, what a sad sight. To my left there was a man in his thirties, but he looked more like he was in his seventies and must have weighed about six stone, obviously a smack head. He was sat next to this ugly beast of a woman. I'd say she was not a day over seventeen, they were holding hands.

On the other side of the room, there was a guy texting away on his mobile. He looked on edge, waiting for something or someone. The guy looked over at me and gave me an evil look.

I realised what the landlord was implying, when he told me to take a seat with the rest of them. He thought I was also some sort of druggie, waiting for my fix.

Ash was their dealer, but I knew that already, as long as he didn't deal in anything other than weed I hadn't got a problem.

The next twenty minutes went by slowly, Ash was late. I decided to give him a few more minutes and then I was out of there, before I caught something. Just then Ash walked in.

'What you drinking?' I stood up and walked to the bar.

'I'll just have a coke please.'

'Fucking coke, surely you want something stronger than that,' I said.

'Of course I do, but the manager knows me, and he knows I'm underage. But guess what, I've only got three days to go and I'm eighteen. Happy days!'

I arrived back at the table and the guy, who was giving me the evil eye earlier, was sitting in my seat talking to Ash. I pulled up another stool and sat down.

'Have you got any?' the guy asked.

'No mate, there's nothing about. When I get some I'll let you know.'

The odd couple overheard what Ash had said and left the bar, leaving just the three of us as the only occupants.

'For fuck sake man, I've been waiting for you to text me back all day and now you say you haven't got any. You lying cunt, I bet you've got some for yourself.'

'Mate, I haven't got any. You'll be first to know when I get some, alright.'

'Come on man, don't give me that shit.'

That's when I butted in. It was obvious to me, this bloke had no intention of leaving until he got what he wanted.

'He said he hasn't got any, now clear off.'

He stood up and looked down at me, with a face like thunder.

'Was I talking to you? Who's this, your fucking dad?'

## The Goat Killer

I stood up, to face up to him. Who the fuck did he think he was talking to. Ash butted in and handed him a bag of weed.

'Here, that's all I've got, it's a ten bag, take it.'

'You see, you see, I knew you were lying to me. Cheers.'

He then turned to me, and waved the bag of weed in my face.

'Sorry mate, I didn't mean to get nasty, no hard feelings.'

He put his hand out for me to shake. I shook his hand not realizing he'd spat in it when I wasn't looking. He smiled at me exposing his rotten teeth.

It only took one punch and he was out cold. I leant over him and wiped my hand on his hoodie top. I picked up the bag of weed and gave it back to Ash, who looked at me open mouthed. By now the landlord had come over asking us what had happened.

'This scum bag was selling drugs in your pub, mate.'

'Was he?' The landlord looked confused.

'What are you, a fucking copper or something?' he asked.

'It's ok Barry, the guy was asking for it,' Ash said.

Rotten teeth started to come round, when the landlord lifted him up and helped him outside.

'Why did you do that? I can fight my own battles thanks, and he was one of my best customers. You can't go around knocking people out, especially not in here anyway.'

'Why, what's so special about this place?'

'It's owned by AK.'

'AK... I've heard that name before. Who the fuck is AK?'

'Trust me, he's a guy not to be messed with. He and his brothers pretty much run the drugs scene around here. That's why this place is still open. Look at the state of the place, he's using it to make his drug deals.'

'Is that who you work for?'

'Me? No way man. I keep myself to myself. That's the big league.'

'How come you get away with selling weed in his pub?'

'AK isn't bothered about a little shit like me, I hardly make a dent in his empire. Anyway, the weed I get probably comes from him. I'm just at the bottom of the layer cake. AK and his gang members run the whole drug scene around here, you name it they deal in it.' Ash lit a cigarette, drew deeply on it and blew the smoke in my face, making me cough. 'Cannabis is their drug of choice, but they also do hard drugs. They have a stranglehold over the city and have done for years. And they've got no qualms about using intimidation, bribery and violence to achieve their aims.'

'How many brothers are there?' I asked, wondering if I'd already met one of them in the form of the loan shark.

'Three of them. Tommy is otherwise known as AK. Colin, his right hand man and Terry, they call him Peanut, because he's got a screw loose. He's got a reputation for cutting peoples fingers off. They call themselves the government.'

'If they've got such a reputation, how come the police haven't arrested them?'

'To do that, they'd need proof, and informants. No one round here would risk saying anything for fear of what would happen.'

'Why, what would happen?' I asked, hoping he'd get to the point. It was beginning to sound like the script of a bad gangster film.

'They'd disappear, like a friend of mine did. AK's girlfriend owns and runs a pet crematorium at his house. Rumour has it, he uses it to get rid of anyone who pisses him off. Whether it's true or not, no one knows.'

I sat thinking about what Ash had said. Could someone really be so evil. I doubt it.

'Did you get the money for the seeds?'

I counted out two hundred and fifty pounds and slipped it to him under the table. Ash went on to tell me the going rate for the seeds he wanted, was ten seeds for twenty pounds. He reckoned he could get a better deal the more we bought. I told him I'd get another two hundred and fifty pounds to him in the next few days.

I sat back for the next hour and listened. This kid knew his stuff. His knowledge of cannabis production was amazing. I'd heard he was the brightest student the college had ever had, now I knew why the college had given him so many chances.

'When's the best time to start,' I asked.

'Now, even though it's early spring, greenhouses quickly warm up in the sunshine. I'd say let's start early so we can benefit from larger plants. Bigger plants mean a bigger harvest, and a bigger profit. We'll be needing greenhouse heaters for cold nights, you can get them from any garden centre.'

I started to make a shopping list. I realised I'd need a lot more money.

'If we can get good soil for the plants and start with good seed genetics, then the plants can grow into true fucking monsters by the end of the grow season. I'll germinate some of the seeds indoors at my old man's house, so it gives them a head start, the rest I'll start straight in the greenhouse.'

'How big are you talking?'

'I've grown in small greenhouses before. Last year I grew one plant that filled the whole greenhouse, and produced several hundred grams of top quality weed. As I said, it's all about the soil conditions; temperature and good care, if we get it right were talking a jungle. When we start, we need to be on it twenty-four/seven, especially in the early stages.'

'We've got a problem. I can cover five or sometimes six nights a week. What happens on the nights I'm not there?'

'That's not a problem. On your night off I'll stay over.'

'Are you sure?'

'I'll be ok, as long as I've got my weed.'

'Ok brilliant, but no smoking the profit when they start budding.' I could picture him stoned out of his head in the compound.

'Someone's got to sample the stuff! Seriously though, we'll have to hang the plants up for three to seven days in a dark room, to let them dry out first, and they'll need curing time. The storage buildings and potting sheds will be ideal for that job.'

We'd been in the Anchor for three hours, the only thing left to talk about now was when we produced our crop, how were we we're going to sell it on. We agreed that, that could wait until another day, but I had a feeling we'd be dealing with AK in the near future.

I made sure Ash got the bits he wanted, heaters, compost, plant pots, and tools, most of it kindly donated by the college. I'd also found sheets of black fabric, which Ash had been pleased about, he said they would help accelerate the flowering. The storage buildings were packed with everything we needed. I was able to give him the rest of the seed money, thanks to me getting paid, which more or less left me broke again

## CHAPTER 9

A couple months had passed, and once we were set up we were well on our way. I had looked on in wonder as the seeds began to grow. The first shoots had appeared just over a week after the seeds were planted, and had grown steadily ever since. With the CCTV in the vicinity of the compound out of action, it was easy for us to set the operation up unnoticed. We thought it would be best to keep the main gates to the compound padlocked. Our set up was perfect, what could go wrong we thought. We worked out that our crop could be worth around two hundred thousand pounds, wholesale, or more if everything went to plan.

It had been just over two months since I'd last seen Chrissie. I was dying to see her, or was I dying for a shag, if I'm truthful. The problem was I had no money, apart from a few quid, so I decided to go and see Daz, to see if he'd lend me some money. After all he owed me a favour, he was shagging Debbie, but I wasn't supposed to know that.

It had been a while since I'd seen my army buddy, I wondered if he could smile now. It was Daz who had stood on the IED. Even though he lost both his legs, he felt responsible for causing all the casualties. No Daz, it was the fucking Taliban, who were responsible, not you, I told him time and time again.

Daz lived on a canal boat, bought with his compensation money. He called it The Dogs Bollocks, what an address. I climbed on board and rang the bell, his mum answered it.

'Hello love, I haven't seen you for ages. How are you keeping, how's Debbie and the kids?' she asked, as a smile spread across her face.

I loved Daz's mum, she was one in a million. While I was in the army, I used to come home on leave with Daz and stay at their house for a few days. She really looked after me, but the real reason I stayed there was because I had a thing for Daz's sister, Mandy.

'Nice to see you again, how's Mandy?' I asked, hugging her and kissing her on the cheek.

She went on to tell me that Mandy and her new American husband had moved to the US.

'Sorry I can't stop, I just stopped by to drop off Darren's washing. I've got to get home and get his lordships tea ready. You can pop round any time, love. You know where we live.' She picked up her shopping bags and squeezing my arm with affection, got off the boat.

Daz was in the kitchen drawing away as usual, he was a freelance cartoonist, that's how he made his living. He was always drawing cartoons while we were in the army, mainly cartoons taking the piss out of somebody, and that was usually me.

'Long time no see. Help yourself to tea, my mum's just mashed.' Daz said.

'You know how it is, busy as fuck, mate.' I replied, pouring myself a cup of tea.

'Still working at the college I take it? How the fuck, do you put up with those students? It's a wonder you haven't strangled one of them yet.'

'I'm working on it.'

I sat down and faced him. I was beginning to feel a bit guilty about not visiting him until now, when I needed a favour.

## The Goat Killer

'It's good to see you mate. How's it going, what you been up to?'

Daz paused drawing, his pencil held just above the paper.

'It could be better I suppose.'

'Is the cartooning paying off?'

'You're joking, aren't you? You'll never see a rich cartoonist. Most of my clients want you to work for peanuts. Sometimes I think the only reason I get the work is because they feel sorry for me, because I've got no legs. I've got to have some perks I suppose.'

'Don't be stupid, the reason they employ you is because you're fucking good and they know you are.'

'How's Debbie?'

'Same as always. Although I'm sure she's seeing someone else.' I said.

Daz stopped drawing again and looked me in the face.

'What makes you think that?' he asked, looking worried.

I could see I'd upset him, so I changed the subject. It didn't really bother me what he and Debbie got up to.

We carried on the small talk for the next hour. The one thing we didn't talk about was the incident, that was a taboo subject.

'Are you still having those flashbacks?'

'Sometimes, although they're not really flashbacks, more like I go into some sort of dream state when I'm angry. To be honest, I don't have as many now.'

I was lying and Daz knew it, Debbie would have told him.

'What about you?'

'What about me? I'm ok, got used to having no legs now. Well, they're not going to grow back are they? It's just in the morning I have a problem, before I put on the prosthetic legs they gave me, or when I wake up for a piss in the middle of the night. I jump out of bed half asleep, then suddenly I'm reminded I've got no legs and end up flat on my face.'

At that moment I laughed my head off, I couldn't help it.

'What's funny about that, you, cunt?' Then Daz joined in with the laughter.

'Do you still go and see Matt?' Daz asked.

'I pop by when I get the chance, leave him a few beers. He's always good for a chat. What about you?' I asked.

'Been down there a few times, when I can face up to it.'

Daz got to the point. He wasn't one for idle chit chat.

'So, Mickey, what made you come round, you haven't been round for ages.'

I had the feeling he thought I was going to ask him what the score was with him and Debbie.

'Alright mate, you got me. I was meaning to come round anyway, but I was wondering if you could lend me a few quid until payday.'

'How much is a few quid?'

'Three hundred pounds.'

'That's not a few quid. There's a tin under the sink, get it for me will you?'

I fetched the tin and put it on the table, he opened it. There must have been a few thousand in there, in twenty and fifty pound notes.

'Fuck me Daz, this lot should be in a bank.'

'It's my money, I do what I want with it,' was his sharp answer.

He counted out three hundred pounds and handed it to me.

'Cheers Daz, I'll get it back to you with interest.'

'Just spend it wisely. Don't go paying off someone's bloody mortgage with it.'

'What with three hundred quid? I doubt it.'

## The Goat Killer

I know I didn't tell him I paid off Debbie's mortgage, it sounded like she was telling him everything. We got into more small talk until I left. I went straight home, grabbed my gear and told Debbie, I was off for the weekend. She didn't ask where, she knew she'd only get bullshit, and anyway, she only had one thing on her mind, that was seeing Daz.

'When do you think you'll be back?'

'Monday dinner, I'm at work Monday night. Why have you got a problem with that?'

'No, even if I did it wouldn't matter.'

## CHAPTER 10

I arrived at London St Pancras station around seven that night. This time there was no Chrissie there to greet me, I'd come unannounced. I thought I'd surprise her, or at the back of my mind the niggling thought that maybe I'd catch her at it with Giles, or someone else. What did I know, she might have a string of boyfriends? All kinds of thoughts were going through my head.

I was now on the underground train on my way to her flat at Golders Green, on the Northern line. I was reading a free paper that someone had left on the seat opposite. On the back cover there was a feature on gardening tips, and a picture of a greenhouse. It reminded me I needed to phone Ash to make sure everything was ok.

'Ash, it's Mickey.'

'Where are you?'

'London for the weekend.'

'Lucky you, guess where I am? I'm sitting in one of the poly tunnels having myself a fat one.'

Ever since we started growing the crop, Ash had more or less camped out there, it was either that or go home and get a hard time from his old man. Things had changed between Ash and his dad. His dad now had a girlfriend and she'd moved in, it didn't take long before she started ruling the roost. It didn't help that she was an alcoholic who got violent when she was pissed.

'How's my babies?' I asked.

'Our babies are doing just fine. I'm telling you now, we're going to have one hell of a grow mate, it's sick.'

'That's what I like to hear. I'll be back Monday, then we can discuss how we're going to get rid of it all.'

'Don't worry. I spoke to one of my mates who knows AK. He reckons he can get us a meet with the main man. I think he'll be up for it, there seems to be a lack of weed around at the moment.'

'Let's talk about it when I get back. See you Monday.'

Speaking to Ash and listening to what he had to say, put me in a better mood. I had a little chuckle to myself, "set up a meeting with the main man." What a twat I thought, sounded a bit over the top to me, he'd been watching too many gangster films. Little did I know the next few months were going to be one hell of a ride.

I soon arrived at Chrissie's flat. Walking up the stairs, I wondered how she'd react to me turning up unannounced, something I'd never done before. I knew she'd be home, as she didn't work evenings. I got to the door and I could hear Chrissie laughing and telling someone off.

'Get off me, stop it, stop it, that hurts.'

Suddenly I was in a rage, I was right, the dirty slag was seeing someone else. I felt like crashing through the door, but I held back. I rang the doorbell, Chrissie was taking her time to come to the door, so I rang it again, this time continually. She opened the door and smiled, I barged past her. All I had on my mind was finding the bastard.

'Mickey, what's wrong?' she asked, seeing the thunderous look on my face.

'Where is he?'

'Where's who?'

'Don't fucking come the innocent with me Chrissie.'

I searched the kitchen, bedroom, toilet, even the cupboards, then I looked down at my feet and there he was, Harvey her kitten.

'Is that who you were looking for?' she said, bending down to pick him up.

If she wasn't mad at me before, she was now.

'For Christ sake Mickey, who did you think I had in here?'

'Sorry...'

'Fuck off!"

'I'm really sorry. I thought...'

'I know what you thought.'

I slipped my arms around her waist, hoping she'd forgive me. She looked away.

'Chrissie, look at me.'

She turned her head and faced me, but she didn't try to pull away from me, that was a good sign.

'What?'

'I'm sorry, but what do you expect? When I heard *get off me, stop it, stop it, that hurts*, I assumed someone else was in here with you.'

She smiled and started to chuckle. I knew I'd been forgiven.

'You are such an idiot!'

Seconds later we were kissing, stripping each other's clothes off. By the time we got to the bedroom we were naked.

'Harvey needs feeding.'

'Fuck Harvey, Harvey can wait. Harvey's had his fun with you, now it's my turn.'

'Don't you like my pussy then?' She said teasing me.

'I'll show you how much I like your pussy,' I growled.

I slid down her body and spent a while getting to know her pussy really well, there were no complaints. I kissed my way back up her body, then kissed her neck, she loved that. Then I started to nibble her neck, she liked that even more. It was too much for her, her breathing became ragged, and

## The Goat Killer

she tried to push me away, then I entered her, and she collapsed underneath me. I was inside her for ages and came a couple of times. We just kept going and going it was amazing. After our shag marathon we sat up in bed, she lit up a cigarette and we chatted.

'So how come you didn't tell me you were coming, trying to catch me out were you?'

'No, I missed you.'

'You mean you needed a shag.'

I turned my head towards her and gave her a puzzled look. Of course she was right, she was always right, but deep down I really did miss her.

'Why are you talking like that Chrissie, just after we've had such good sex.'

'Chill out babe, I'm just playing.'

'No you weren't, what's up?'

'Good sex, that's the problem. We didn't make love, did we? I never know where you are, what you're doing, when I'm going to see you next, or if you really love me. Am I just a fucking shag?' she asked, as tears filled her eyes. 'I'm just about fed up with the situation, Mickey. I want you, I love you, I want to spend the rest of my life with you. I've got the feeling that will never happen. In fact, I know it will never happen. I know nothing about you, do I? You've never spoken about your mother and father, brothers, sisters, where you come from, where you're going, for all I know you could be married.'

I sat looking at her, where had all this rubbish come from? Someone had been filling her head with shit, and it didn't take a genius to figure out who.

'Are you married?' she asked, looking straight at me.

'Of course I'm not married.'

I sat there in silence while she continued her barrage of abuse, there were tears streaming down her cheeks. I felt sorry for her, she looked to me for answers, answer's I didn't have for her.

'Surely you can give me something. You won't tell me anything, will you? You turn up when you want, out of the blue, expecting me to open my fucking legs.'

'Do you want me to leave?'

'Is that all you can say? Yes! Fuck off, now you've had your shag, go.'

I started to put my clothes back on expecting her to change her mind, but she didn't. She just lit another cigarette and stared out of the window. Now I'm feeling awkward and really guilty.

Yes, I had used her for sex, but she enjoyed it. It was more than just sex now. We were crazy about each other. Chrissie wanted to take it to another level, the problem was I wasn't ready for that. If she knew the real me, would she still be interested, I doubt it, it would destroy her.

I left without saying a word, and in a way I was glad, after that dressing down, it would have been hell.

## CHAPTER 11

I sat on the train with my head tilted against the window so I could see through the reflection of the lit carriage. Looking out at the street lights, my mind was doing somersaults thinking about Chrissie. I think it might be time to let go, the girl deserved better than me, maybe it had already happened, that could be the last time I'd ever see her.

The only other person in the carriage sitting in the seat adjacent to mine, was this old guy. He must have been in his early seventies. He wore a veteran's badge on his blazer. I smiled and nodded.

'You were in the Guards then? I recognise the badge.'

'Twenty-two years in the Guards, 1961 to 83. What about you, have you ever served in the forces?'

'Yes I did. I'm out now, I left two years ago. I did ten years, loved it.'

'How come you got out, then?'

'It's a long story. Twenty-two years... I bet you've seen a thing or two.'

That was it. It was pull up a sandbag for the next hour. He told me his name, Bobby Hardy. He reminded me of Derek, and boy he had some stories to tell. It sounded like he'd been through some shit.

The next thing I knew we were pulling into Leicester station. I'd fallen asleep, it was now twenty past eleven and the old fellow was still rabbitin' on. Just then, as if from nowhere, three youths entered the carriage. One sat next to Bobby, the other two opposite. They'd obviously been out on the piss, the noisy bastards. I wasn't happy they'd disturbed my sleep. It wasn't long before they started on Bobby.

'Fucking hell lads can you smell piss?" said the guy sitting next to Bobby.

'It' must be that coffin dodger sitting next to you, Andy.' One of his friends replied.

'Fuck me, it is you! You, dirty old bastard. When was the last time you had a bath? You stink.'

The old man just sat there taking the abuse, staring out of the carriage window. I was already weighing up my options, should I intervene now, I thought. I decided to bide my time. They carried on giving the old boy more abuse, then the one they called Andy, a six foot nothing, streak of piss, took Bobby's hat and put it on his head.

'Can I have my hat back, please?' Bobby asked.

'What hat... you mean this hat? This is my hat.'

'You better give it back or...'

'Or what old man, what you going to do, old man?' The one called Andy asked, as his friends sat giggling at his antics.

'Give him his fucking hat back and get off the train.' I said, finally losing my temper.

They all looked over at me, surprised by my outburst. Most people would turn a blind eye to their antics, but I couldn't.

'You what?'

'You heard. Give him his fucking hat back and get off the train.'

'Who the fuck, are you? You get off the train.'

'Last chance.'

Andy stood up and headed for the toilet, leaving me a passing comment.

'I suggest you keep out of it you fucking knob. You better not be around when I get back.'

## The Goat Killer

I let him leave the carriage. Then I stood up and headed in the opposite direction, his two friends smiled at me thinking I was heeding their mate's advice. I left the carriage, walked down the platform, and jumped back on the train opposite the toilet Andy was in. As this piece of shite came out of the loo, I grabbed him, put one hand around his throat and forced him up against the toilet wall. I started to squeeze his neck, he began to kick out. I buried my knee as hard as I could between his legs. I think his bollocks were now in his throat, because he started to talk in a higher pitch. I took out my mobile phone with my other hand and took a picture of him.

'What are you doing, why are you taking a picture of me?'

'It's just a little hobby. I like to take pictures of my victims before and after.'

He looked worried.

'After what?'

'After I've fucked them up and finished with them. The pictures are just my little trophies. Well fucking smile then.'

For the next thirty seconds I made this guy pay, he'd disrespected a veteran, someone who put their life on the line for their country. You could say I was doing my bit to educate him in respect.

Meanwhile, back in the carriage the old man was still being victimised by Andy's friends. I walked back into the carriage, gave Bobby his hat back and took my seat. The two yobs looked puzzled, they looked round to see where their buddy was.

'Where's Andy, what have you done with Andy?'

Like a scene from a horror film, their brave mate's bloodied, fucked up face appeared in the window. He then proceeded to slide down the carriage's outside wall and collapsed in a heap on the platform. Maybe I'd gone too far, my intention was to just give him a slap, but I couldn't stop beating him. As the train started to pull away, his mates couldn't leave the carriage quick enough.

'Thanks son,' Bobby said.

'That's ok pal, he deserved it. They should have had some respect. I've probably done them a favour, they'll think twice next time.'

For the rest of the journey I returned to staring blankly out of the window, all I could see were street lights. We were about to pull in at Derby station, I looked over at Bobby, my new friend.

'You're awake then? You've been asleep since we left London,' he said.

'What about what just happened. The three lads that came on at Leicester station?' I asked.

'Son, we didn't stop at Leicester station.' The old man answered, looking puzzled.

I looked at my phone for the picture I took of Andy's battered face, there was nothing there. Come to think of it, why the fuck would I take a picture of my victim? I'd dreamt the whole thing. Shit, I thought, the dreams are getting worse.

## CHAPTER 12

I arrived back home around midnight, there were no lights on in the house. Had Debbie gone to bed? She often went to bed early, because of the kids getting up around six every morning, she'd probably been in bed hours. Thinking I wasn't coming back until Monday dinner, the kids could be at her mum's while she was round Daz's; or he could even be lying next to her in our bed. That would be funny, he'd shit himself if I walked in on them.

I let myself in, being careful to not make a noise and wake anybody up. I walked into the kitchen and opened the fridge to see what there was to eat, not much, she hadn't been shopping. I just cut myself a large chunk of cheese, sat down and ate it, then washed it down with a large glass of milk. I took out my phone and texted Chrissie, I tapped in the words sorry xx, I didn't know what else I could say at that moment. It's up to her now, if she doesn't reply that's fine, I ain't no fucking bunny boiler.

I thought it would be best if I slept on the sofa, like I'd been doing for the last few weeks, but I needed to go upstairs and take a piss.

I tiptoed up the stairs and arrived on the landing to be greeted with a baseball bat, full on, straight in my face, I fell to my knees. As I looked up everything became dizzy, Debbie was standing there looking shocked, bat in one hand, with the other hand over her mouth.

'It's you… shit I'm really sorry.'

The next minute I was back in Afghanistan, laying on my back in the Chinook, with Daz and Matt each side of me. I was the only one who was conscious.

'You're going to be fine pal, just relax.'

'Are they ok?'

'Your two buddies? Yes, pal they're going to be ok.'

'Mickey, my name's Mickey.'

I woke up lying in Debbie's arms.

'I know your name's Mickey, you, daft sod,' she said, hugging me and stroking my face, where it was beginning to swell.

I started to come to my senses. I couldn't believe what had happened.

'What the fuck did you do that for? You fucking psycho. Hold on, is this another dream, am I dreaming?'

'No you're not dreaming. I've just hit you with a baseball bat. I'm really sorry. God, what have I done, shall I call an ambulance?'

I struggled to get to my feet and entered the bathroom. I stared in the mirror for a damage report. My face was already swelling up on the right side, plus I'd lost a tooth, and three more that were more or less hanging out. I decided to check how loose, they were, they just wobbled a bit, but stayed where they were. The pain was unbelievable. Debbie started to cry. I barged past her and headed downstairs, I couldn't deal with her tears at that moment.

Heading back to the kitchen, I washed my mouth out and bit on a clean towel to stop the bleeding. Debbie stood in the doorway, a look of fear on her face.

'I thought it was him coming back.'

*Him* meaning her ex, I just nodded my head. I suppose I only had myself to blame, after all, she wasn't expecting me back yet. After a while the bleeding stopped, but the pain hadn't subsided.

'Let me have look.'

I opened my mouth. She winced as she saw the damage she had caused.

## The Goat Killer

'You need to see a doctor and get checked out. Shall we head for casualty?'

'No, it'll be alright, what can they do anyway, they can't put the tooth back can they?'

'I don't know? They might be able to, they can do wonders nowadays.'

'Just go to bed, Debbie, I'll be alright. I've lost a tooth and got a swollen jaw, I've had worse.' I took a couple of painkillers and laid down on the sofa, waiting for them to kick in. My jaw hurt like hell.

It was a rough night, I hardly got a wink of sleep. I slept in. It was ten o'clock by the time I woke up, Debbie was out. It was the first Saturday of the month, the day she normally had her hair done. Back when we were dating, she'd have her hair done every Thursday, she wanted to look nice for when I came home on weekend leave.

I looked in the mirror, it wasn't as bad as I thought, the swelling had gone down, but my jaw still ached like hell. Debbie had done me a big favour, that tooth needed to come out, it had been giving me jip for years, and I hated the dentist. My tooth got extracted, but not the way I imagined it to be. I took a few more pain killers and chilled, I had the rest of the weekend to recover, I wasn't at work until Monday evening. I decided to give Ash a call to see if everything was ok with the weed. After the shit I'd been through in the last twenty-four hours, I wanted to make sure nothing had happened to the grow.

'Ash, what's happening?' All I could hear was gun fire. 'What the fuck. Ash are you there?'

'Everything's cool, no worries.' he answered.

'What's that racket?'

'I'm watching a kick arse film on my tablet. Listen, we need to talk.'

'I'm at work Monday night. Once I've locked up the campus, I'll come down to the compound, we'll talk then, unless it's urgent.' I answered, hoping nothing had gone wrong.

'Monday's fine.'

'Ok, see you later.' I said, feeling relieved.

I checked my phone to see if I'd had a text off Chrissie. Nothing. Fair enough, I thought, it was my own fault. She deserved better, I kept telling myself. I don't think I realised how much I felt about her, but I'd thought the same about Debbie at one time. I suppose you have to move on, maybe if I strangled another goat it would help me get over losing her.

The best time I had with Chrissie was when we went to Tenerife for a week, it was a last minute deal, and a surprise. We had such an amazing time, we didn't want to come back. On the plane back home, we made a promise that when her modelling career was over, we would buy a villa out there and live there for the rest of our lives. She would run a clothes shop and I'd have my own little bar called Mickey's place. That was four years ago.

I fell asleep for few hours and awoke to the sound of Debbie arriving back from the hairdressers; she'd also been shopping. I complimented her on her hair, I always did even if it looked crap.

'Thank you,' she said. Perhaps she didn't expect such kindness after the previous night.

She emptied her shopping bags into the fridge-freezer and filled the kettle.

'Coffee?'

'Go on, then.'

'You look awful.' She said, gently caressing my bruised cheek.

'I'll live.' I replied, as I tried to smile.

'About last night...'

'Forget it. I don't want to talk about it. You did the right thing, what if it was him?' She threw her arms around me and hugged me tight. I couldn't really blame her for what she had done to me.

# CHAPTER 13

Before I knew it, the weekend had come and gone. I arrived at work on Monday night at 6pm for my night shift and relieved Sam. He shot off as soon as he saw me coming up the drive. I think I worried him a little bit.

I completed my lock up of the campus without any problems, most of the college was empty. It was the start of the summer break and the college would be shut down for the next eight weeks. The only people on site would be security and a few staff, no students thank god. I made my way down to the compound, it wasn't long before I could smell the weed.

'What happened to you? You look like you've been hit with a baseball bat,' Ash said

'Maybe I have,' I said, then went on to tell him what had happened. He just laughed at me.

'Jesus Christ, it stinks around here.' I said, as a sweet smell tickled my nostrils, making me sneeze.

'We're not growing fucking lettuces here you know.'

'I see you've been busy.'

Ash had placed more fencing and shrubs around the compound. It was beginning to look like a garden centre.

'It was just stuff lying around, I thought I'd make use of it. I wanted to make sure the place was more secure, inaccessible to unwanted visitors and invisible to prying eyes. Nothing I can do about the smell though, and it will get worse, ten times worse. This lot should start flowering next month.'

'Really, that early?' I asked surprised.

'I told you that black fabric would help accelerate the flowering.'

'So how long, when will it be ready?'

'About six weeks. Yep, about two weeks before the new college term starts I reckon, then we can start harvesting.'

'I'm sorry I haven't helped you that much. I'll be here most nights during shutdown, and anyway I've used all my holidays up.'

'No worries, I'll grow it, you sell it. I don't think we'll be able to smoke all this lot ourselves. We might be in luck, the word on the street is that weed is hard to get, after a spate of police raids in the area. So we might be able to get rid easy, and for a good price.'

'Who are we selling it to?' I asked, although I could guess the answer.

'AK, the guy I spoke about in the pub. There's nobody else around here who'll buy this much weed. Unless... you know anyone? I think he'll bite your arm off for it. My betting is he'd rather buy it off us, than line the pockets of the Romanians, who charge a fortune for smuggling it in, and most the time the stuff's low quality.'

'How much do you think this lot will be worth?'

'One plant could yield anything from twenty-five grams to seventy-five grams or more. Let's go on the average, fifty grams per plant. At a street value of ten to fifteen pounds per gram, one plant could be potentially worth five hundred to seven hundred and fifty pounds. We have around three hundred plants, so our yield could have a street value of one hundred and fifty to two hundred and twenty-five thousand quid, but I think it will be more, a lot more.' Ash said, grinning like a Cheshire cat.

My face started to ache, I tried to smile, but it was too painful. After chatting to Ash for another ten minutes, I left to go back to work. The night shift went quickly, I finished work at six in the morning, and like ships passing in the night, Debbie got out of bed and I got in, and that's the way it was for the next few weeks.

## CHAPTER 14

I got up at one in the afternoon and went to visit Matt. I dropped him off his usual few beers, and then headed back home. For the rest of the day I chilled out, it was now four o'clock. Debbie arrived home from having her hair done, it was like ground hog day. I knew what we were having for tea before she said anything, the smell was making my mouth water.

'I bought you fish and chips,' she said.

We sat down at the kitchen table and ate. Usually Debbie was too busy eating to talk, but today she was quite chatty. I had to leave for work in an hour, so I zoned out, I wasn't interested in the petty gossip she was repeating.

'I had a visitor this morning.' Debbie said.

'Oh yeah,' I said, suddenly alert to what she was saying.

'Some guy asking about you.'

My ears pricked up, 'who?'

'I don't know, he didn't say, he just asked if Mickey lived here.'

'And what did you say?'

'Yes. I told him you were asleep, as you'd been at work all night as a security guard at the college.'

I shot up out of my chair. Who the fuck was asking questions about me?

'How long ago was this?'

'About nine o'clock this morning.'

'Shit, why didn't you tell me?' I asked. My stomach began churning.

'You were asleep, for fuck's sake. What have you done?'

'What did he look like?' I asked, hoping it was someone I'd recognize.

'Blonde hair, early thirties, tall, he talked like a snob. He was wearing a check jacket.'

'Did he say anything else?'

'All he said was he was an ex-army mate, and he was just passing though. He was ever so nice. I told him I was your partner and he said I had lovely children.'

I grabbed my pack up, put my coat on and dashed out of the door. The description didn't fit anyone I knew and that worried me. Debbie shouted up the garden path.

'Where are you going, don't you want your fish and chips? Suit your fucking self.'

I headed straight to the college. Thoughts of what Debbie had said spun through my mind. Who could it be, an ex-army mate, I doubted it, the police may be, sniffing around? I bet Ash has grassed me up. Shit, surely not I thought. One of AK's gang must have got wind about the grow. My mind was doing somersaults trying to think who it might be. I arrived at the college and the gatehouse.

'What are you doing here, you're early?" Sam asked, looking surprised.

'Have you had anyone here asking questions about me?'

'Come to think of it, yes, about an hour ago. He asked where you were, I said you had the day off, then he asked me how long you'd been working here for.'

'What did you say?'

'I told him you'll have to ask him that. I didn't tell him anything, he was a right smarmy twat. No offence if he's one of your mates, but he looked and sound like a copper to me.'

'Good lad, you didn't let him on campus did you?'

'No, he wasn't interested in coming on site, who was it anyway?'

'I don't know, but if he turns up here again, phone me will you?' I said, scribbling down my mobile number and handing it to him.

I watched Sam as he walked down the drive, then pulled down the barrier and locked the main gate, locking myself in. That was the advantage of being on the night shift, no arseholes around telling you what to do.

I carried out my first patrol of the campus, then decided to visit Ash. I always texted him before I walked down the track. He had deliberately planted thorny plants round the compound, it was really effective protection. That effective I struggled to find the hidden entrance myself. Ash had made me buy five big blackberry plants. It had been a messy job to carry them down to the compound. At the end I was so prickled that it looked like I had spent the night shagging a hedgehog.

He'd done a proper job, there was absolutely no way that anyone could guess cannabis plants were growing here. The only give away now the plants were getting bigger was the smell, and today it was particularly strong.

Ash crawled out of the hidden entrance, he was starting to look like a weed plant. The reason for the stronger than usual smell was obvious, Ash was smoking the biggest spliff I'd ever seen.

'Come on in, follow me,' he said.

I followed him crawling along the ground through the hidden entrance, and came out surrounded by dozens of budding cannabis plants. Ash had made himself a cosy little hideaway, complete with hammock, gas stove and television. He even had a blow up armchair. There was everything he needed and most of all weed. We sat down and he offered me a drag of his spliff.

'No thanks, I don't do drugs, especially not on duty.'

He started to laugh at my ironic answer. I joined in with the laughter after realising what I'd said.

'This weed I'm smoking, I'm not kidding, it's fucking awesome. Here have some.'

I shook my head. My mind was fucked up enough already, without taking drugs.

'I don't have to smoke it. I can taste it just sitting here. So what do you think, have we hit the jackpot or what?'

'We've not only hit the jackpot, we've smashed it. Just look these plants. Some of the plants are two metres tall and a metre wide. With some of them, I've had to remove a few panes of glass. They've grown that tall, they've outgrown the fucking greenhouse. I think it's time we started harvesting, some of the plants are ready now.'

'How long will that take?'

'God knows. On my own a few weeks, but I'll sort that out. I can get a couple of my cousins Steph and Katie to help us out.'

'Hold on a minute, I don't like the sound of that.'

'Chill out... Blood is thicker than water, trust me. I'd trust those girls with my life, they've helped me before. They know what they're doing and anyway, it's going to be hard work harvesting this lot. Who else can we get to help, college students? I'll put an advert in the local paper if you want.'

'Don't be a twat, if you say they're ok then I'll go with that... I think.'

'Along as they get a bag of weed each, and a few quid at the end of it, they'll be happy.'

'More importantly, how are we going to sell it? There's too much here to sell straight to retail, it would take us years. We need to move it on, sell it wholesale as quickly as possible,' I said.

'Like I said before, I'll get a meeting set up with AK. I'll put the word out to the right people. The good news is, weed is still hard to get at the moment... well, the good stuff like ours. I heard there's some crap out there, people don't want it, they'd rather wait or go out of town.'

'So how much do you think we've got?'

'It's looking like we can easily get over a hundred grams per plant. So this lot could have a street value of at least three hundred thousand pounds or more.'

His answer brought a smile to my face.

'When AK realises this stuff is the best around, he'll bite your hand off for it. Just be careful if I do get this meet with him. I've heard if you cross him, AK can be one evil bastard, capable of having someone killed. Violence, or the threat of violence, is part of his business.'

'Don't worry about me, I'm not scared of him. I've come across worse people than him, but it won't come to that, we'll do a deal, everyone gets what they want and everyone's happy.'

I left Ash in his weed heaven and headed back to the gatehouse, I had lots to think about. Should we really let outsiders in on our secret? I suppose he's right, we have no choice, I don't know anyone apart from Debbie and Daz and they haven't got a clue what I'm involved in.

I hadn't heard from Chrissie in weeks. I thought about her every day, but I was beginning to think me and Chrissie were now history. I wasn't going to text her, it was like a chess game and it was her move, she'd checkmated me. I had nothing to give her, but I was still here if she wanted me.

A few more days went by, it was my day off and I was ready for a break. It was a hot day the temperature must have been in the mid-eighties. I filled up the paddling pool for the kids and set up the barbeque. Debbie's mum and step-dad were coming round. I'd also invited Daz, but I doubted he would turn up. It was midday, when out of the blue I received a text from Ash, saying he'd set up the meet with AK, and I was to meet him at the Anchor in thirty minutes. I downed tools and told Debbie I had to go, that I'd be back later.

'What do you mean later, how much later?'

'I don't know, an hour or two.'

'What's so important that you have to go just like that?'

I was half way up the street and I could still hear her bitching. I didn't have time for a shouting match.

I arrived at the Anchor and walked into the bar looking for Ash, then I checked the lounge, was this a wind up? Ash was nowhere to be seen. After ordering a coke with loads of ice, I asked the barman if Ash had been in.

'No, I haven't seen him, mate,' he said.

His body language told me he was lying. I took my drink and went to sit outside near the main entrance. I tried to phone Ash, but there was no answer. I decided I'd wait another ten minutes, then head home. I was just about to leave when a black BMW pulled up, about three metres away from me, it had tinted windows. The driver's side window lowered slightly.

'Are you Mickey?' Came a voice from the car.

'Who's asking?' I said, as I stood up and walked over to the car cautiously.

'Are you Mickey?'

'Yes,' I answered.

The guy I was speaking to was well built, had short cropped hair and his face looked like he'd been in a few scrapes, he just looked dead ahead.

'Get in the car, someone wants to speak to you.'

'No, it doesn't work like that. You watch too many movies.'

'AK wants to speak to you.'

'Where's Ash?'

'Get in the car. If you want to see your mate, I suggest you get in the car.'

I opened the rear door expecting to find a couple of heavies, but it was just him on his own, there was no one else. I climbed in the back. The car spun off down the road. A few minutes later, we'd driven past the college and into the countryside.

'Where are we going?'

'You'll see.'

'Is Ash ok?'

'He's ok.'

'Not much of conversationalist are you?'

He looked at me through the rear view mirror, like I was a piece of shit. Ten minutes later we pulled off the road and up a driveway. We came to a halt in front of electric gates. After a few seconds they opened to let us in. I noticed two Rottweiler's sitting panting on the lawn. I could see a big house further up the drive, with some kind of water feature in front of it. I assumed this was AK's place, this guy must have money, a lot of money. We drove into a large garage-like building, the electronic shutter closed behind us. The driver got out and opened my door. I got out of the car to be greeted by another one of what assumed was AK's heavies. I recognised him, he was the loan shark I'd confronted at Debbie's house.

'So, we meet again, my name's Colin, I'm AK's brother. I've got to frisk you. Don't worry, I'll be gentle, unless I find anything,' he said, as he pushed me back against the car.

'Go ahead, I ain't carrying anything.' I replied, through gritted teeth.

The driver folded his arms, leaned back against the car and smiled at me.

'Does your twin brother fancy me or something?'

'He's not my twin, but he is my brother, his name's Peanut.' He answered, spinning me round and slamming my chest into the side of the car.

He carried out the rest of his search roughly and then I was invited into the house. I followed Colin out of the garage, and up a path to the house. That's when I saw AK for the first time, standing in the doorway. He looked like he was in his mid-forties, six feet tall, balding and very tanned. He was wearing a pair of white shorts and a Fred Perry pink polo shirt, a thick gold chain around his neck and chunky gold rings adorned several fingers.

'Mickey, we meet at last,' he said.

AK shook my hand, it was a firm grip, I think he was trying to make a point.

'Come this way,' he said, indicating I should follow him into the house.

He led me to what I assumed was his office. A large desk stood in the centre of the room, bookcases lined two walls and several chairs stood around the desk. I watched as he made his way over to a large globe atlas.

'So what's your tipple? I'm having a Bacardi and coke,' he said, lifting the top of the globe up to reveal a well, stocked bar.

'I'm ok thanks. Where's Ash?'

'Ash... Ash is fine, he's in the pool enjoying himself, we'll join him later. Are you sure you don't want a drink, how about a coffee, tea?'

'Go on then, I'll have a cup of tea, NATO style.'

'NATO style, I know what that means, white with two sugars.'

'Correct, so you were in the forces then?'

'Nah, too much of a naughty boy. My dad was, he used to say that all the time. He was an ex- military policeman.'

'Nice one, I bet you were proud of him.'

'Not really, he was a cunt. He used to beat us all the time.'

I wondered if those beatings had given him and his brothers brain damage, they all seemed like nutters to me.

'Lisa...Lisa,' he shouted at the top of his voice.

Lisa was AK's bit of stuff. She walked in through the patio doors.

'Darling be an angel, could you get our guest a cup of tea, white, two sugars.'

Lisa. In her mid-thirties and drop dead gorgeous, was wearing a bikini. She needn't have bothered, it hardly covered anything.

'A bit of a hero then Mickey, so I hear, Afghanistan veteran. I bet you've seen a few things.'

This guy knew everything about me, where I lived, who I socialised with, my injuries, everything. He even knew I travelled down to London a lot. I knew Ash couldn't have told him, he knew nothing about my past. AK had certainly done his homework on me, I tried not to look surprised.

'So it was one of your boys asking all those questions about me. That's a bit out of order, sending your people round my house and where I work.'

AK gave me a stern look.

'You're mistaken young man. We don't work like that. The information was given to me freely. Your girlfriend Debbie has a lot to say.'

I looked at him questioningly, he took a sip of his Bacardi and coke and smiled.

'Facebook Mickey. It's amazing what you find out by logging on. Modern technology, isn't it great. How's your jaw by the way? Pretty handy with her baseball bat your Debbie. How's her ex, didn't she nearly take his head off one night?'

'He deserved it, he shouldn't hit women.'

Lisa arrived back in the room with my tea, as she walked past him he slapped her backside.

'No you shouldn't hit women, unless they like it.'

Lisa didn't flinch, but I could tell she didn't like it, and from the look on Colin's face he didn't approve either. She gave AK a dirty look as she placed my tea on the table.

'Nice, isn't she. Lisa put some fucking clothes on, will you?' AK shouted as she left the room.

'How do you know Debbie that well?'

'I don't I know her personally. I know her ex, CJ. He used to work for me.'

'Let's get to the point, shall we,' I said.

'Yes, I think we should. I found out the other day that your friend Ash has been asking questions, too many questions. Telling everyone and his fucking dog, that you and Mister Mouth wanted to meet me. So, you can imagine,

I couldn't wait for him to tell me what he had to say and find out what it was all about. That's why I invited him to this lovely house of mine, don't you think it's a lovely house, Mickey?'

'Yeah, it's great.' All paid for with drug money no doubt, I thought.

'Let me tell you, I couldn't believe my ears when he told me you both had some top quality merchandise to sell. In fact, a lot to sell. Then he produced this bag of weed for me to sample, which was very kind of him. Personally, I don't touch the stuff, but I've been informed by one of my associates that it is like he said, top quality, isn't that right Colin?'

'That's right AK,' Colin answered.

'I'm a businessman, naturally I'm going to be interested. I couldn't pass up this opportunity, but here's where I have a problem. Being a businessman my time is precious, and if there's one thing I hate, it's some scrawny little cunt wasting my time, get my drift? Have you really got a large quantity of weed stashed away, or is he talking bollocks, Mickey?'

AK began to move towards the door, I'd entered the room through.

'While you think about your answer, let me give you the guided tour.'

We left the house and headed in the direction of the garage. Walking past the garage, we followed a path on the other side. Up ahead I could see a large square building and wondered where I was being taken.

'This is the legitimate side of my business operation,' he said, opening the door and entering the building.

I looked around the room, it resembled the chapel at the local crematorium, then I remembered the conversation I'd had with Ash. AK led me through a door on the far side of the room, to show me where the pets were cremated. I had the feeling he was trying to unsettle me. It didn't work. Leaving the building, we retraced our steps.

Arriving back in the house he poured himself another drink. I was about to answer his original question, and had only uttered one word when he stopped me with a wave of his hand.

'Let's carry on this conversation by the pool, shall we?' he said.

We walked through the large patio doors and I followed him in the direction of the pool. When we reached the edge of it, I looked down. He was right, Ash was in the pool, but the pool was empty, apart from Ash, tied to a chair and gagged.

'I take it this is your friend? You seem an honest man and I'm a pretty good judge of character. All I want you to confirm to me is that you have over thirty kilos to sell. Is that correct?'

'That's right, it'll be ready in a few weeks' time.'

'Where is it?'

'What do you mean, where is it? I'm not telling you that. I'm not that fucking stupid.'

Just then one of his gang members appeared, holding two very hungry looking, barking Rottweiler's on a lead.

'Our dogs haven't eaten for a few days. If you value your friend's life, I suggest you tell me where it is. Don't worry, you'll receive the going rate, I give you my word.'

Ash began to fill the pool up, but it wasn't water. I was angry, but I knew I had to keep my cool and not go into one of my dream states. Keep your cool Mickey, you've been in worse situations than this, I said to myself.

'As far as valuing my friend's life, for one he's not my fucking friend, two I don't give a shit whether Ash becomes dog meat and three I suggest you back off. My boys know exactly where I am and if anything happens to me this place will be turned into a fucking war zone, and it won't be nice.'

For a few second there was deadly silence. AK just stared at me expressionless, and then he laughed. I'd called his bluff and won. He called the dogs off, but left Ash where he was, he put his arm around me.

'Come on soldier boy, let's talk business.'

I sat with him for another half hour. To be honest, I began to warm to him a bit, but I knew that underneath his friendly exterior there was pure evil.

He asked me about my time in the army, I told him just a few basic things. I wasn't prepared to tell him everything. He went on to tell me how he got the name AK.

He was living in London at the time as a high ranking gang member in another firm. He got an eight stretch for being in possession of a firearm, an AK47, along with a large bag of cocaine in his boot. A rival drug gang had set him up. In prison, he got labelled with the name AK and it stuck. He was out after six years and decided to make a fresh start up in the Midlands, where it was quieter and people wouldn't know his face. He now hated Londoners with a vengeance, even though he was a London boy himself.

We started to talk money and after a lot of haggling, we settled on six pounds a gram. Me and Ash would make one hundred and eighty thousand in total. He was getting a good deal. I knew he would double his money, but I wasn't bothered. We agreed to meet up when we were ready to deliver. Me and AK had completed our business when Ash appeared, looking like a scared rabbit.

'Did you enjoy yourself in my pool young man?' he laughed.

Ash didn't say a word, he just stood there shaking. The poor fucker had been scared to death, and it had affected him. I joined in with the laughter.

'You're not scared of me, are you?' AK asked.

I paused before I answered. Was this another one of his stupid tests?

'No, I'm not scared of you. I'm not scared of anyone.'

'Then we might have a problem.'

'If we get our money and you get your weed and everyone's happy, then there won't be any problems will there? Happy days.'

'Good man, that's how to do business.'

'We'll be in touch when it's ready.'

I stood up and we shook hands. AK instructed Peanut to take us back to the Anchor pub. Sat in the car we didn't say a word, but I could tell Ash was still in shock.

Later, back in the pub we sat in the corner, the landlord placed two pints of John Smiths on the table.

'I didn't order any beer,' I said.

'No these are on the house, AK's paying,' he replied.

'That's kind of him, cheers. Fuck me, he even knows what beer I drink.'

'Yeah, until he falls out with you,' Ash said.

It was the first time he'd spoken since the swimming pool incident.

'I told you, you can't move around here unless he knows about it. I want to ask you something. Would you have let those dogs attack me? You said you didn't give a fuck about me, I've never been so scared in all my life.'

'I was calling his bluff. I didn't want to appear weak.'

'You didn't answer my question.'

'Let me see... nearly two hundred grand's worth of weed or your arse...That's a no brainer, isn't it?'

Ash looked confused. Maybe his meeting with AK had upset him more than I realised.

'Of course I wouldn't have left you for the dogs, you, idiot.'

I told Ash I had to get home, I was having a barbeque. I invited him, but he declined. I think he wanted to go home and change his underpants.

## CHAPTER 15

Everything was set, the deal was done, the weed was nearly ready, what could possibly go wrong now. Well, just about everything. It all started when I received a text from Chrissie out of the blue.

*'I'm texting you because you're not worth talking to, you fucking arsehole. You lying bastard, you've lied to me from the day we met. I can't believe you've used me all this time, Mister fucking security guard, sorry, Mister married security guard with two kids. How could you do this to me, does she know about me? I bet she doesn't. The only thing I've got out of this relationship, is a lesson never to trust men again, goodbye and good riddance, never, I mean never, contact me again, wanker.'*

Well, that told me. I suppose I deserved all of that. In a funny sort of way, I was relieved the truth was out, and now it was obvious who the mystery person was, Giles, unless she had hired a private dick. It must be him, it fit his description. I'd love to spend five minutes alone with him right now, the sneaky bastard.

I sat for a while thinking about it all, it was over, time to move on. Come to think of it. Who could blame the girl for sending Giles up here, to spy on me.

The next few weeks went by quickly. We were now only few days away from the harvest. AK had been in touch, asking Ash when it was going to be ready. The boy just told him he'd be first to know.

I still had lots of things to worry about. How we were going to get the weed out of the college, and delivered to AK was one. More important where was the deal going to take place, and who called the shots. Ash was busy doing his bit and more. I'd hardly done anything so far, now it was my turn.

I was back on my night shift. After locking up, I wandered down to the grow, to see Ash.

The smell was really bad, we needed to get this lot bagged up and quick. It was still shut down, but the college would be open for business in a week's time, we couldn't have timed it better.

I climbed through the entrance, Ash wasn't alone this time, there were two topless girls there with him. They were all sat down in a circle, facing each other smoking weed. They'd been busy bagging up the crop, all three of them were dirty and sweaty.

'Did you know the college run a strict health and safety policy here?'

'For Christ sake, man! I wish you'd warn me when you were coming,' Ash said, jumping up.

'Aren't you going to introduce me then?'

'This is Steph and this is Katie. Girls I'd like you to meet Mickey, my business partner.'

The girls were just that. They couldn't be much older than nineteen. Steph was short with dark hair and a little overweight. Katie was tall and thin, with blond hair.

'Hi Mickey, why don't you join us. We were about to have a threesome. You could make it an orgy,' Katie said, laughing.

I wasn't expecting that. I wondered just how reliable the girls were.

'Take no notice of Katie, she's a bit forward,' her friend said.

'Can I have a word, Ash?' I said, not too happy about the girls being involved.

The boy came to stand beside me. Nodding my head towards the concealed entrance, I started to walk away. We went for a walk a short way down the path, away from the girls.

'Are you sure the girls are ok?'

'Yes, the girls are sound. They wouldn't cross you after what I've told them…'

'Why, what have you said?' had he made me out to be some kind of monster, I wondered.

'You know, that you were in the army. The way you dealt with AK. Nobody speaks to him like that.'

'How do they know AK?'

'They used to be his girls.'

'What do you mean his girls?'

'His girls, street dealers, you know?'

'Tell me you're having me on.'

'Chill out Mickey. They don't deal for him anymore, they're free agents. That was when he first came on the scene, before he made it big.'

'You're certain you can trust the girls?' I asked, still not convinced.

'Yeah, sure. Just say the word, and I can sort you out with one of them,' he said smiling. 'Steph is really nice, or even both of them.'

I got really mad and grabbed Ash around the neck. I began squeezing and just stared at him. My mind was blank.

'Mickey, you're hurting me.'

I squeezed harder. At this stage I'd usually go into some sort of waking dream, but I didn't. Eventually I let go, my arms dropped to my sides. Ash was coughing, holding his neck. I could see the two girls peering out of the hidden entrance, they looked on startled, wondering what was happening.

'What the fuck was that about? It was as though you weren't here. You were on another planet, man.'

'Sorry… it's just a little problem, I thought I'd sorted it. Obviously I haven't. It won't happen again.'

'Go back to your work girls, everything's ok,' Ash said, spying the girls.

'Why didn't you tell me you had a problem? You must have gone through some shit in the army.'

Deep down I knew why I reacted like I did, the Chrissie situation had affected me. I'd lost the person I cared about most, but hold on, this time I didn't go into a dream, like state. Was that a good thing?

'How far have you got?' I asked, changing the subject.

'I reckon we'll be ready in three to five days. We'll definitely have it all bagged up by Monday.'

'Brilliant. Monday's a bank holiday, there'll be no one around.'

'One of AK's boys phoned me this morning, they were hassling me. They wanted to know when we'll have the weed ready. He said they've got a good place for the exchange.'

'Just keep stalling them, they can wait, and yes, I've been thinking about the drop off. I want it on our terms, for some reason I don't trust them.'

I waved to the girls as I was leaving, there was no response. I'd obviously scared them, but maybe that was a good thing.

I completed my shift and walked home, popping into Naz's shop for a newspaper on the way.

'Morning, Mickey,' Naz said with a cheerful smile on his face.

I wasn't in the mood for a chat. I picked up my paper and turned to leave. He tapped me on the shoulder, I turned sharply out of instinct, I think I scared him.

'What?' I said.

'I need to give you something.'

Suddenly, Nazim appeared to be dressed as an Afghan civilian.

'What, information? Don't give me any crap this time. That information you gave me last week turned out to be bullshit.'

'Are you ok?' he asked in a quavering voice.

'Of course I'm ok. Give me the information.'

'The guy who was looking for you last week, he left this.'

He handed me a business card. I was back in the real world, and Naz was now hiding behind the counter. I'd obviously scared the shit out of him. And I thought the dreams were over. The business card was a Retro Fashions card, with Giles's name on the front and the word user underlined several times on the back. I walked out of the shop looking at the card, then screwed it up and threw it on the pavement. As I left the shop, I heard the door being locked behind me.

When I got home, Debbie was already up and about, I refused her offer of a coffee and went straight to bed. I lay there awake for hours, thinking about Chrissie and what I'd love to do to Giles. Fuck 'em, move on Mickey, I thought. Eventually, I got to sleep around ten. I was up again at four that afternoon and got ready for work. That was the worst thing about working permanent nights, ground hog day again, time just flew by, it could get really depressing.

## CHAPTER 16

It was now Friday. I arrived back at work to find Sam half way down the drive walking towards me. He couldn't wait to tell me something.

'Hey, the site manager is on site.'

The site manager had been on holiday for the last two weeks, it was his first day back.

'So what?' I couldn't make sense of the words.

'I went for a wander down the back track to the old compound earlier. When I got there I could smell something really strange. I got on the radio and told Dave Sherwood. I think the smell was cannabis, I know that smell, I've smelt it before.'

'Let me get this straight, you told the fucking site manager?'

'Yes, he's on his way down there right now,' Sam said with an uneasy smile on his face.

'Don't say another word. Just grab your stuff and get out of here,' I said, trying not to lose my temper.

'Have I done something wrong?'

I'd now backed him up against the security office door, my face was inches away from his. I really wanted to rip his head off, the wanker.

'I won't tell you again, for your own safety, grab your stuff and leave.'

A voice I hated came over the radio. I had no choice, I had to let go of Sam. I'd never seen him move as fast as he did at that moment. He ran down the drive like an Olympic sprinter.

'Security, are you receiving? Security, are you receiving?' the radio squawked.

I picked up the radio in slow motion. Dave Sherwood was the last person I wanted to speak to.

'Receiving.'

'Can you meet me down at the compound, and bring the keys please.'

'Roger, on my way.'

What the fuck am I going to do now. I picked up the keys and headed for the compound, trying my hardest to think of a way out of this situation. I was screwed, we were about to lose everything. Arriving at the compound, the site manager stood there, arms folded, with a serious look on his face.

'Can you smell that?' he asked.

'Smell what?' I feigned ignorance.

'It's cannabis, the place reeks of it. What the hell has been going on in there?'

Fuck me, give the guy a medal. The racket he was making would alert Ash.

'Open it,' he demanded.

I tried the lock, it had rusted up and wouldn't open.

'I'm sorry, it's been locked for months. I think it's seized up.'

He pushed me to one side and took the key from me, then tried himself. This was my moment. As I moved behind him, I picked up a large piece of metal, which was lying on the ground. Before I could knock his head off with it, I heard the lock click open, he turned and smiled.

'We're in,' he saw the lump of metal I was holding, his face changed. 'What were you going to do with that?'

I didn't lose my coolness, 'I was going to force the lock open.'

He opened the gate, made his way through the overgrown foliage. He was lost for words. He couldn't believe his eyes.

'I need to phone the police. I can't believe this is happening right under our noses.'

Out of the corner of my eye I could see the white of Ash's eyes, deep in the forest of plants. Most of the plants had been harvested. A week before it would have been even more spectacular. I had to think fast, what could I do? I had to make a decision. All that hard work was about to be ruined by this wanker. He started to phone the police on his mobile.

'Hold on. I wouldn't do that if I was you.'

He looked at me like I was a mad man. I could tell he was angry by the way his nostrils flared out.

'What are you talking about, this is serious.'

'Think about it, the college term is about to start. I can see the headlines now, *Cannabis College shut down.* The press would have a field day, nobody will want to send their kids here, we'd all be out on our arses. A sensible person would inform the principal first. Let him make the decision.'

'I suppose you've got a point,' Sherwood said

'I'm sure he'll thank you for it, in the long run.'

'You're right. I'll phone him in the morning. He arrives back from his holiday at lunch time tomorrow.'

We made our way out of the compound. Ash watched silently from his hiding place.

'Lock this gate and I want regular patrols all weekend. Let's hope we can catch whoever's responsible. Tell Sam well done, for alerting me to this.'

He disappeared up the track and out of sight. Ash and the girls appeared from the side entrance.

'What now? We're screwed. We're nowhere near finished yet.'

'How long do you need?'

'At least another two days. We have to find somewhere to stash it. What're we going to do? Do we take what we can and call it quits? You should have hit him with that lump of metal, while you had the chance.'

I told Ash and the girls to work faster, and I'd be back down to see them later. I had all night to think about what I was going to do. Back in the gatehouse I paced up and down for hours. I thought about everything, as it normally does, it came to me. I went down to tell Ash.

'I'm going to phone Sherwood up and tell him the police are down the compound. As we walk back down the track, I want you to jump out of the bushes, and cave his head in with a shovel, then we can put his body through the wood chipper.'

Ash stood there open mouthed.

'Have you lost it?'

'It could be a bit messy, I agree. How about we burn his body in the boiler house?'

'Are you serious? This is not Afghanistan, where killing people was just part of your daily task. This is civvy street.'

'I was joking. We only have one option, and that is to kidnap him until we've done the deal, then when we've all gone our separate ways, we can let him go. He's not telling the principal until tomorrow. I know where he lives. Tomorrow morning we'll break into his house, tie him and his Missus up for a couple of days until we're finished.'

'Hold on a minute did you say *we*? Correction, you can kidnap them. I'm not cut out for stuff like that, that's your department, I need to stay here and carry on harvesting this lot.'

'It's the only plan I've got, unless you can think of a better one.'

The rest of the night shift went slowly. I couldn't stop thinking about the next morning. I had to get there early, before they got up, and hardly anyone was around. I thought hard, searching for a better idea, there wasn't one, "Operation Sherwood" was on.

## CHAPTER 17

I arrived home the next morning; Debbie and the kids were fast asleep. I changed quickly, putting on my old combat jacket, jeans, and a balaclava. I put masking tape in one pocket, a hammer and rope in the other. Five minutes later I was on my way. What the fuck was I doing? What a mess.

Sherwood lived about a mile away, I could get to his house easily without being seen. There was a track through the wood at the end of our garden, which lead straight to the rear of his property. Within ten minutes I was there. Sneaking through the hedgerow and behind a wall next to his property. I saw he'd left a downstairs window open, this was going to be easy. I was ready, I was going in.

Suddenly I could hear a vehicle, it was a police car pulling up outside his house, then another. Shit, the game was up. Sherwood must have told the police, all that hard work, up in smoke, I couldn't believe it. I started to walk back through the woods and home. I tried to phone Ash to warn him, but there was no reply. The college was probably crawling with police more like, Ash was in custody, I'd be next, great. My head was down, I was gutted.

I arrived home and sat in the living, waiting for the knock at the door, the police would surely want to speak to me. As the security officer, they'd want to know why I hadn't noticed that there was a huge cannabis farm on the premises, the game was up.

Debbie entered the room, I gave her the scare of her life, she ran out of the room, then peered around the living room door at me.

'Is that you?'

I was still dressed like a serial killer, combat jacket, balaclava, with the rope, tape and hammer placed on the coffee table in front of me, looking like I was waiting for my next victim. I was lost for words, what could I say.

'What the fuck have you been up to?'

Was this one of my weird dreams, was I really dressed like this, just back from attempting to kidnap someone? No, it wasn't a dream, it was real alright. I couldn't be arsed to speak to her.

'I worry about you. I think it's time you made an appointment to see the doctor. You're not right in the head. If you don't make the appointment I will.'

I stood up and walked past her. My night shift from hell had drained me. I needed to sleep.

'I'm off to bed. Wake me up around two.'

I lay in bed thinking about everything, maybe Sherwood had done me a big favour telling the police. Kidnapping was one step too far. What the fuck was I doing even considering it, in fact what was I doing getting involved in drugs in the first place? Doing deals with gangsters, what had happened to me? I've fucked up the job, my girlfriend had dumped me, my best mate was shagging my ex missus behind my back. My only mate is an eighteen, year old, kid come drug dealer. Is this what I've become? One thing had changed for the better, most of my flashbacks had stopped, why? Was it because I was back in the thick of it? I thrived on this shit. I didn't have a very good sleep, I tossed and turned for ages. It felt like I'd been in bed five minutes when I heard Debbie shouting me from downstairs.

'It's two o'clock.'

'Cheers.'

'You need to get up. You'll never guess what's happened.'

What the hell is she talking about. I came to my senses, and remembered the predicament I was in. I wandered downstairs, I didn't know what to expect. I sat down at the kitchen table. Debbie handed me the local paper, with my coffee. The headline reads *FATAL CAR CRASH ON A52*. I began to read the article. *College site manager, Mr D Sherwood, from Wood Oak, was killed instantly, in a head on collision with a heavy goods vehicle, at around 6.45pm yesterday.* I started to smile.

'Yes,' I said, as though my favourite football team had just scored a goal.

'What you smiling at and what do you mean yes? You're sick, the guy's dead. Isn't that your boss?'

'I'm not smiling.' It didn't matter how hard I tried to stop it, my lips were curling with happiness.

'You look like you've won the bloody lottery. God knows what goes off in that head of yours.'

'That's sad that is, that's really sad,' I said, holding up the newspaper. I was biting my lip, trying to stop myself from laughing.

'What is up with you, didn't you like him or something?'

I'd got my mojo back. I put the paper down.

'What're we having for dinner? I fancy fish and chips.'

The rest of that afternoon, I felt like a massive weight had been lifted off me, everything was back on. I headed for work an hour early.

'You get earlier every day,' Sam said.

'Yeah, it's the missus, she's doing my head in, you know how it is. You can go Sam, I'm here now, anything to tell me?'

'Did you hear about Dave Sherwood? He was killed in a car crash last night, not long after he left this place. I couldn't believe it when I heard the news. By the way the principal's, on site, he said he'll be on site until seven.'

'Is he, in his office?'

'I think so.' He said nodding his head, as he gathered his stuff together.

It felt like two steps forward, three steps back. Had Dave Sherwood told the principal? Surely not. I locked the gatehouse up and took a wander over to the principal's office. As I walked through the reception, I bumped into him on his way out.

'You can lock up, I'm just leaving. I suppose you've heard about David, shocking news, isn't it?'

'How did you find out, sir?'

'He was on the phone to me when it happened. He left a message on my voice mail.'

'Oh my...' I had to find out if he had said something.

'All he said was, *I need to speak to you urgently* and then the line went dead. I've checked and it was very close to the time the accident happened. I don't suppose you know what was so urgent?'

'No. When he left here yesterday, he seemed cheerful.'

'Very worrying. I need to tell the police about the call I think.'

'I wouldn't, if I was you, sir. With the first day of term on Tuesday, the last thing you need is police all over the college.'

'You're probably right. You won't say anything about the phone call?'

'Me? No, sir,' I zipped my lips

'Good man, have a good evening. Oh, by the way, there's a strange smell hanging around, can you find out what's causing it please,' he said as he walked towards his car.

'Will do.'

I went back to the gatehouse, raised the barrier and the principal left site. I took a large intake of breath, realising how lucky we'd been. It was time to check on the weed and find out how far we had got. I sent Ash a text to let him know I was on my way down. When I arrived at the compound, he was waiting outside looking worried.

'Is it sorted?' he asked.

'He's dead.'

A look of horror crossed his face.

'His car got totaled by a lorry last night,' I said, handing him the paper to read.

'Looks like someone up there is looking out for us.' A smile lit his face.

Ash and the girls were almost there, we needed to get the gear off site as soon as possible. The problem was where do you hide thirty kilos of weed?

I needed to get my head straight. I headed back to the gatehouse, made myself a cup of tea and sat pondering. After a while I had my plan. It was a long shot, but if I could persuade Daz to help me. It would solve all our immediate problems, storage, transportation and delivery. I needed to see him. I texted and told him I'd be round the next day at around one.

## CHAPTER 18

The night shift went quickly, I was struggling to keep my eyes open. It was four in the morning, and Ash knocked at the gatehouse door.

'All finished, all bagged up and ready to go.'

'How much have we got?'

'Pretty much what I said. I've given the girls five ounces each, they're well happy.'

'Where are they now?'

'They're asleep. I'm going to join them in a bit, I'm fucked.'

'Get them to hang around, we might still need their help.'

'Where are we going to store it?'

'I've got a good friend Daz, he has a canal barge moored up at the marina around a mile away. With the compound backing on to the canal it's the perfect way to get it off site. I'll get him to pick up the gear tomorrow night, and store it on his barge until we sort out the drop. It can be somewhere along the canal bank.'

'That's perfect. Can this Daz be trusted? He's not going to sail off with our weed is he?'

'He's my best mate, we served together. There's only one drawback.'

'And what's that?'

'I haven't asked him yet.'

It was now Sunday, I got out of bed early, around noon, there was no sign of Debbie and the kids. She said she was going round her mum's. I got ready and headed for Daz's.

How the hell was I going to convince him to help me out, this was well out of his comfort zone. I know he likes his weed, but not thirty kilos of the stuff, and getting caught would get us banged up for a very long time. In the army we'd take risks without thinking about it, he was nearly as crazy as me. But now things were different. I knew what buttons to press, plus I had my ace card, I was desperate.

I arrived at the canal barge and climbed aboard, there was no one around. I tried opening the hatch, it was locked, so I began to call his name. Daz's head popped up out of the hatch. He didn't look happy.

'What the fuck are you doing here?'

'Didn't you get my text?'

'I told you before, I hardly ever check my phone.'

'Aren't you going to invite me in, I'm here now.'

He looked a little on edge. It took him a few seconds before he answered.

'I'll put the kettle on.'

I stood in his galley kitchen while he made me a coffee. I was amazed how well he had adapted to his new legs. It must be a challenge living on a canal barge with his disablement, but it didn't surprise me, Daz was always a fighter. We sat down to talk; I told him everything. He couldn't believe what he was hearing.

'Why have you gone down this road, what do you need the money for?'

I told him all about Chrissie, and if I wanted to get back with her, I needed the money to keep her happy. She wasn't the main reason, but I wasn't ready to tell him all my plans.

'I knew there had to be a woman involved. Why didn't you just tell her the truth, mate?'

'I was going to, but I was worried she might dump me, and now she has anyway? She's the best thing that ever happened to me, since me and Debbie got together the first time.'

'Mental Mick the craziest bastard, I've ever met. The man who could take on the Taliban single handed, not scared of anything. It's amazing isn't it, what women can do to a man. So if this Chrissie has dumped you, why do you think she'll take you back? Talk away mate.'

'I can't explain it, but I know she will. This is my mission, I started it so now I have to finish it, and anyway, there are other people relying on the money. I could do so much with the money, it will help me get back to where I want to be.'

'And where's that? You can't go back in the army. I don't think you know what you really want. Sorry, I can't help you, I'm done with risk taking. Look at me, the army took my legs, now you want to take away my home. What the fuck would I get out of it?'

'You'd be helping a mate. I'd do it for you.'

'No. I can't help you.'

'Fair enough, no problem I understand.'

There was silence for a while, then I decided to take a different approach.

'Didn't you say you needed another fifteen grand, to finish paying for the barge? Maybe I can help you there.'

'I'm not listening.'

'Just a few days. One final mission and the barge could be yours.'

'It's a narrow boat and I don't need the money.'

My plan wasn't working it was time to play the ace card. I didn't want to do it, but it was my only hope of getting him to help me.

'I know about you and Debbie.'

That grabbed his attention. He didn't say a word, he just looked at me worriedly. Although me and Debbie were no longer a couple, for Daz it was a betrayal of our friendship.

'I've known about it for a while mate.'

'I don't know what you're talking about.'

'You know exactly what I'm talking about. You two have been an item for a while haven't you? Unless I'm fucking delusional. Come on mate, you're talking to Mickey, you're seeing Debbie aren't you?'

I heard a noise, coming from the bedroom.

'Have you got visitors?'

I got up to open the door. Daz put his head in his hands the game was up. Debbie was sitting on the bed half-dressed. She looked at me, her face was expressionless. Putting on her top, she joined us at the table.

'We were going to tell you, weren't we Debbie,' Daz said, looking to Debbie for support.

After we were hospitalised in Birmingham following the incident, she came to see us both every week. I got released back to my unit and Daz convalesced at his mum's house. She started to go round to see him and things developed from there.

'I knew all the time. I was just wondering when you were going to get round to telling me.

'Who's this Chrissie and what's the drugs thing?' Debbie asked.

'I take it you heard everything?' I said.

'That's who the black bags were from,' she said.

'Black bags?'

'That guy who was snooping around asking questions about you. He dropped some black bags off, full of your gear, mainly clothes. The word *user* was written in big letters on a large picture of you and her.'

'Why didn't you tell me?'

'You were on edge. I didn't tell you for all sorts of reasons, I suppose. How could I confront you when I was seeing Daz, and by the bloody way, me and Daz were aware you knew about us. It was obvious. You and your bloody mind games.'

Debbie wasn't as daft as I thought she was.

'A cannabis farm. What the fuck have you been doing, have you lost the fucking plot Mickey?'

Now everything was out in the open, everyone knew everything about everyone. I got up to leave, there was no point in hanging around. Just as I got to the stairs, Daz spoke.

'How many days do you want me to hide the weed for?'

They couldn't see my face, I had a smile like a Cheshire cat.

'I don't fucking believe it. Daz don't tell me you're going to help him,' Debbie said.

She got up and put on her coat, she wasn't happy.

'Where you going, Deb?' Daz asked.

'Where do you think? I'm going home. I don't want to see you two again until you've both come to your fucking senses, or this deal, whatever you want to call it, is over with. It wouldn't surprise me if I'm visiting you both in prison,' Debbie said as she left.

'It looks like you've got a lodger Daz, or I should say a shipmate. What time do we sail?' I said, offering him my hand to shake.

We both laughed, it felt like the old days, he would be watching my back. Daz smiled and shook my hand.

I went back to Debbie's to get some of my stuff. I didn't want to be around when she arrived back with the kids. I headed back to The Dogs Bollocks for the rest of the afternoon. We sat and planned everything, as much as we could plan. There was still the matter of setting up the meeting with AK, but for now it was all about getting the weed off campus.

## CHAPTER 19

I walked up the drive to the college; Sam was outside the gatehouse waiting for me.

'Evening,' he said.

'Got anything to tell me?'

'Yes, I've been down the compound and that smell has gone now. It must have been a few kids messing around smoking weed.'

'You're probably right, I'll keep my eyes open.'

In the early hours of that morning, The Dogs Bollocks had arrived at the compound. There was an old mooring point, we had no problem loading the weed on board. The gear was off site it was a massive weight off my mind.

All that was left in the poly tunnels and greenhouses was Ash's campsite, where he'd been existing for the past few months. We chopped what was left of the plants up into small pieces and burnt them in an old metal dustbin. Any plants we missed could be dumped in the surrounding bushes. Ash had done the business, he'd played his part, now it was my turn.

I woke up later that day to the sound of the narrow boat's engines, I was gagging for a cuppa. Wearing only my boxer shorts, I made my way up the stairs to the deck. The sudden daylight made my eyes squint and then came a barrage of abuse from Daz, who was at the wheel.

'The boat stinks. I want this stuff off my fucking boat today, and get some bloody clothes on will you.'

I didn't recognise where we were. It definitely wasn't the place where we'd been earlier.

'Where are we? Why are we moving?'

'We're travelling down the canal, away from the marina.'

'Why?'

'Because thanks to you, The Dogs Bollocks is full of weed. My mum was coming to see me this morning, but I had to put her off. I couldn't bring her on here, people were starting to complain that the whole marina smelt of cannabis. It was only a matter of time and the police would have been sniffing around, that's why. This boat is like a giant spliff.'

He didn't shut up for the next thirty minutes. I just shut the hatch and left him to moan at himself. I needed to think straight. The first thing I had to do was tell the security firm I worked for I was sick. I needed a few weeks off to sort this out, and anyway, I wouldn't be needing this shit job anymore once the money came rolling in. I decided to phone them straight away.

'That's right, yes, I'm ill... What do you mean what's wrong with me? I'm fucking ill, that's all you need to know... I need to send you a sick note, listen you don't pay sick pay, so why should you give a shit. I'll tell you what, shove your fucking job. I quit.'

That was the end. I was now unemployed and after that outburst, unemployable. It felt great, no more fucking twelve hour shifts on minimum wage.

By now I was dressed, Daz had stopped the boat and anchored up. We sat at the table drinking coffee. My mate wasn't talking. I could tell he was still pissed with me. I told him I'd jacked my job. It didn't go down well. He began giving me a lecture about responsibility, I suppose I should have expected it, he'd always been the one to worry about the future.

'Ok. I'll get the deal set up today.'

'You better, or this lot's going over the side mate.'

I spoke to AK on the phone and arranged to meet him at a supermarket car park in Derby, at four that afternoon. I was told to come on my own.

I arrived early; I sat in a burger restaurant looking out of the window for AK's black BMW. It arrived. It sat there for a while, then it left and then it came back. I suppose they were making sure they weren't being followed. I received the miss call I was waiting for. I ate the rest of my cheeseburger and made my way to his car. I heard the central locking click and took it as my signal to climb in the back.

AK was sat in the front passenger seat, his second in command Colin was sitting in the back, side on so he was facing me, his driver Peanut just stared at me in the mirror like before. I felt intimidated but I tried not to show it.

'Mickey, how are you?'

'I'm fine, thanks,' I said talking to the back of AK's head.

'I was just saying to Colin, you've met Colin haven't you, of course you have.'

Colin just smiled and nodded his head, chewing away on his chewing gum. I noticed he had one hand hanging down in the foot well, he was holding something.

'I was saying to the lads the other day, that we hadn't seen Mickey for a while. I said don't worry, he'll turn up. I told them I trusted you, and guess what, as if by fucking magic you're here.'

'Why wouldn't I be? I'm a man of my word. I'm ready to do the deal.'

'And what deal is that? Remind me.'

'I've got some gear to sell.'

'Have you?'

'You know I have.'

'That was then, Mickey. Things can change on a day to day basis in this business, can't it Colin? You see Mickey, I don't need your weed anymore.'

'You told me you wanted the gear, and we made a deal. It was a hundred and eighty grand, for thirty kilos that was the deal and now you're telling me the deal's off.'

'No, I never said that, did I? I'll tell you what I'll do, only because I like you, Mickey. I'll give you ninety grand, for the lot and that's it.'

'I don't know who the fuck you think you are. The deal is a hundred and eighty that's it. If you don't want the weed then fuck you, I'll find someone else to sell it to. And by the way, you lot don't scare me, I've dealt with bigger fucking apes than you lot.'

I felt the barrel of a gun on the side of my head. AK turned in his seat to face me.

'Are you threatening me, Mickey? I hope not, we were getting on really well.'

'You're going to shoot me in the middle of the fucking supermarket car park, at the busiest time of the day, with CCTV camera's everywhere. Surely you're not that stupid.'

'No Mickey, we can go on a little trip. I'm sure we can find a nice out of the way place to do that.'

'I left strict instructions; if this vehicle leaves the car park, one of my boys will be straight on to the police, telling them I've been kidnapped by armed gangsters in a black BMW with the number plate AK471,' I said, hoping I'd get out of this alive.

AK started to laugh, like he'd heard the funniest joke ever.

'Mickey, you kill me! He's good, isn't he boys? Do you really think I believe you? I'll tell you what, you've got some, balls. Put the gun down, Colin. Ok, you can have your hundred and eighty, when and where?'

'I'll text you a meeting place at six tonight, bring the money and you can have your gear.' I didn't trust him, but my options were limited.

'You have a deal,' he leaned over and shook my hand.

'Let him out.'

Peanut released the central locking and I was out of there. I stood there expressionless, and watched them drive away. I'll be glad when this deal's done, but somehow I knew this wasn't going to go smoothly. It was time to get my team together. I phoned Ash and told him to meet me at The Dogs Bollocks, and to bring the girls with him.

# CHAPTER 20

I had a rough idea how I was going to play this, but now AK had tried to double cross me, the rules had changed.

I spent the next ten minutes in the supermarket, buying what I needed to make this work. It took me a while to get back to the boat moored near a lock at a place called the Bubble. This stretch of the canal ran between open fields. There were no other boats around. Ash arrived with the girls and I briefed everyone.

We were going to meet up with AK at Barrow bridge, a short distance from the Bubble, when I was a kid I used to go fishing there with my mates, and I knew the place well.

There was a lay-by near the bridge which lead down to a stone path under the bridge. There wouldn't be anyone around at nine at night, it was an isolated spot, and it was far enough away from the nearest property for us to go unnoticed.

I sent a text to AK. I told him where the deal would take place. A short while later he replied, saying he agreed with my choice. He said they'd turn up in a black electrician's van with gold lettering, the deal was on.

We all took our places on the boat for the journey to Barrow bridge. Ash and the girls were a bit nervous, but me and Daz assured them everything would be ok, as long as they did as, instructed. It took us about an hour to get there. We stopped under the bridge and waited.

We didn't wait for too long, at nine sharp we could see headlights in the distance, a few seconds later a van pulled up, which fitted the description I'd been given earlier.

'What now?' Daz asked.

'Shush, let them make all the moves.'

We heard the sound of the driver's door open and shut, then the sound of a sliding door opening. We could make out three figures, climbing down the bank towards us.

'What a stupid place to meet up, there's nettles everywhere,' we heard one of them say.

'Evening boys, where's AK?' I asked.

'He doesn't come on these sort of trips,' Peanut said as he drew near the boat.

As far as they were concerned, it was just me and Daz on the boat.

'Right. Let's get this over and done with. Where's the merchandise?' Peanut asked.

'Where's the money?' I replied.

He passed me a grip, I passed it to Daz. It looked like the money was in five grand bundles, of fifty pound notes. He disappeared below to begin counting it.

'I hope it's all there, gents, like we agreed,' I said.

I hoped AK would be true to his word, but you could never be sure. I started to pass over the bags of weed, they made a chain from the boat, up the bank to the van. I'd got to twelve bags when Daz appeared.

'There's no way there's a hundred and eighty grand here, it's well short.'

'Explain,' I said, 'the agreement was a hundred and eighty, where's the rest?'

'There ain't no rest.'

Peanut pulled out a handgun. I'd been expecting some kind of double cross after what had happened earlier in the day.

'There's ninety grand there. Take it, that's all your getting, think yourself lucky.'

'No way, you only get half, if you want the rest of it, I suggest to cough up the other ninety grand.'

'This isn't the supermarket car park at the busiest time of the day, this is a canal bank in the middle of nowhere. If I have to I'll shoot you. Hand over the rest of the weed now.'

'We might be in the middle of nowhere, but you're surrounded.'

*Surrounded* was the code word for the others to appear. Ash and the girls sprang up out of the hatch, wearing heavy black tops and balaclava's, pointing their weapons at the three men, who were now startled.

'Take it easy guys,' Peanut shouted.

'Come on Peanut, let's get out of here,' one of the gang said.

'You need to listen to your buddies Peanut. I suggest you take your weed, put it in the van and go. If you want the rest of it, come back with the other ninety grand.'

'AK isn't going to like this, Mickey.'

'I'm quaking in my fucking boots. I don't give a shit what AK thinks. It was him who went back on his word. He can't bully me. You can tell him that too.'

They left without saying another word and we were on our way. The plan was not to go back to the Bubble, we travelled on. One hour later we were all sitting in the main cabin of the narrow boat, staring at the large pile of money in front of us.

'I've never seen that much money before,' Ash said, as he sat looking in awe at the pile of notes.

'It's a pity it's not all of it.' I answered.

'They'll be back,' Daz said.

'I know, but we're half way there. I need a strong drink.'

'The toy guns worked a treat, they fell for it hook line and sinker. Where did you get them from?' Katie asked.

'The supermarket, £6.99 for the AK47's and £4.99 for the Uzi.'

'That's a cracking deal that, did the job though, they worked a treat in the fading light. Did you see their faces? They shit themselves,' Ash replied.

'I'm thinking we were the one's shitting ourselves,' Daz answered.

'Still, nobody's hurt. Now all we've got to do is get rid of the rest of this weed,' I said.

We split the money up, I gave Daz half the money I promised him, six grand and the girls two grand each, leaving me and Ash with eighty grand to split between us. Everyone was happy apart from Daz. We still had a problem, his narrow boat was loaded with cannabis and we needed to shift it asap, before AK came looking for us, but where, that was the problem.

After a long silence, Ash said, 'I reckon we could get rid of most of what's left of the gear ourselves. Leave it with me.'

I didn't know what he had in mind, but it was too late to talk now, it was nearly midnight and we needed to be up early, before AK tracked us down. If we moved the boat every day, we could hopefully avoid his henchmen.

'Let's talk about it tomorrow, I'm fucked.'

We all found somewhere to sleep. I lay on my bed trying to think of what to do next. What will AK's reaction be, maybe he'll leave us alone, especially when his men report back, telling him we were armed to the teeth. He might have second thoughts about coming back. Where could I move the weed to? I didn't have a clue. I was sure by the morning I'd have a plan. Then my thoughts drifted to Chrissie, I really missed her, I wish things could have been different. I started falling asleep, thinking about when we were making love, there were to be no bad dreams that night.

## CHAPTER 21

I woke the next morning at five o'clock, I'd tossed and turned most of the night. I'd got used to being awake all night at work, it was a habit that was hard to break.

I had to get this cannabis off the boat quickly. I ordered a taxi to the college and met up with a confused Sam at the gatehouse.

'What you doing here Mickey? They said you were sick.'

The security firm obviously hadn't told him I'd jacked my job yet. They probably thought I was joking.

'Didn't the college tell you I was picking up one of the maintenance vans at half six?'

'Nobody said anything to me.'

'Tut… that's typical of the college. I'll be a few hours, ok?'

'What do you want it for?'

'I'm going to fill it with drugs then sell them downtown.'

'You crack me up some times. The things you come out with.'

I took the van keys from the key cabinet, jumped in the van and headed back to the boat. Everyone was still asleep.

'Come on you lot get up. We've got work to do,' I called out.

A short while later, the van was loaded with the cannabis, and me Ash were on our way.

'Where we going?'

'Remember Derek, the old boy security guard who died a few months back? He had a plot on an allotment. I often went down there to give him a hand and chill out. Sometimes we just sat and swapped war stories, over a few bottles of his home brew.'

'But the shed might be being used by someone else now.'

'I doubt it. They're closing it down next year, they're building a new housing estate. By the way, it's not a shed. Derek would have gone mental if he heard you say that. It's an old railway carriage.'

We arrived at the allotment, there was no one around. Because of the imminent close down, most of the plots where now derelict. I found the key to the carriage under a barrel, where Derek always left it. The carriage was secure and large, with enough space to store the rest of the weed.

'Look at the size of this place. I could live here,' Ash said.

We soon had the cannabis stashed safely in the carriage, we locked it up and headed back to the boat. On the way, Ash began to explain how we were going to get rid of the rest of the weed.

'We want to get rid of this gear as soon as possible right? This is the way it will work.'

I listened on intently, I didn't have a clue how it all worked. Ash had it all planned out.

'To attract the customers, we'll offer buy-one-get-one-free deals, whether they buy an ounce or a ten bag. If they're end users or street level dealers, it doesn't matter, we take their mobile numbers. Whenever they want weed they just send us a blank text, then our runners are dispatched to make deliveries.'

'Who's going to be doing the deliveries?' I asked.

'Me and the girls, they know what they're doing. They used to deal for AK remember? In fact, they'll know all his customers. Fuck me, he's going to have a fit when he finds out we're dealing on his patch.'

'AK can go and fuck himself, he tried to stitch us up, we're just returning the favour.'

'Other worry is the police. Once they get wind of what's going down on the streets, they'll be on us like a rash,' Ash said, looking worried.

'Yes, but we'll be long gone by then with any luck. The one thing we can't do is tell anyone where the gear is, only me and you need to know.'

'What do you think, shall we do it? It's the only way we'll get rid of it, it's one thing running a cannabis farm, but becoming drug dealers is another ball game altogether,' Ash frowned as he spoke.

'It's only weed for fuck's sake. We just want to make a few quid. Let's just make our money and get the fuck out.'

The next few days, once the word got out that we were practically giving it away, people couldn't get enough. It was selling quicker than I thought. We were all still living on Daz's narrow boat, even though it was starting to piss him off, he put with it. Anyway, he was part of our cartel we kept telling him.

The boat was brilliant for getting round the area, most of the running was mainly done on bikes. We made sure no weed came anywhere near the boat. We even made Ash go for a walk if he wanted a smoke, just in case we were being watched by the police. Everyone had plans for the future and what they'd be doing with their cut. Ash had plans of buying a static caravan, the girls wanted enough money to spend the summer in Ibiza, Daz wanted to pay off his narrow boat then rent it out. We never discussed what his future was with Debbie. I'd told him I was glad they'd got together. I knew he'd look after her. I still had feelings for her, but it was like the love of a brother for his sister.

By the second week we'd got rid of at least half of the drugs, and we'd dragged in another thirty grand. Daz had had enough, he wanted his boat back. I suggested he go and stay with Debbie, and we rent the boat off him until the weed was gone. He was up for it and Debbie was glad he was out of it.

I hadn't seen Daz for a few days, when he turned up out of the blue. Ash and the girls were out doing the business.

'Come to check on your boat Daz? We're still afloat. I quite like this lifestyle,' I could see on his face something was bothering him.

'We need to talk.'

We sat down in the kitchen area. He passed me a creased up note and asked me to read it. It read, 'If you value your life get off my turf, final warning.'

'What the fuck's this about?'

'It was wrapped round a brick that was thrown through the window.'

'Are Debbie and the kids ok?'

'Debbie and the kids were in the kitchen, if they'd been in the living room, I dread to think what would have happened ... I've told her to go and stay at her mum's for a few days. Who the fuck would do that with kids in the house?'

'It's a message from AK, he probably got one of his minions to do it. He's probably pissed off about not being able to find us.'

'When will this be over?'

'Not until we've sold up. I'm not going to let some gangster drug dealer tell me what to do. Come on Daz, we can deal with scum like that all day long, with what we've been through.'

'You are just like him, listen to you.'

'No I fucking ain't. Listen, we'll get rid of the rest of the stuff by the end of the week, and that's it done, I'm out of here and everything will be back to normal ok?'

'If you say so.'

'I do fucking say so. By the way does this mean you're moving back to the boat, surely you're not staying in the house?'

'Somebody's got to look after the place for Debbie.'

'You stay here Daz, after all its your boat. I'll take care of the house. Like I said, it will be all done by the weekend.

Later that night I'd forgotten about the brick incident. Maybe it wasn't anything to do with AK, maybe it was just some local kid who thought he'd be the big man.

More bad news came in. Katie had been knocked off her bike in a hit and run, luckily she wasn't badly injured, just a few scratches and bruising. She said it was definitely one of AK's men, she recognised the car. It was the same car that took me to his house. She told me it was parked in the Anchor car park.

'I think it's time for some retaliation,' I said to Daz.

'I don't think that's a good idea. We know they have guns, what have you got?'

Daz was right, once we start retaliating it will just accelerate. It was now ten at night, I made my way to Debbie's house, hoping by the time I got there I would have calmed down.

My phone started to ring, I didn't recognise the number at first, then I realised it was Chrissie. I'd deleted her number. I got fed up staring at it every time I thought about her. I answered it.

'Hello, it's me Chrissie.'

I was stuck for words. I didn't know what to say. It felt great to hear her voice. I'd missed her so much.

'How are you?'

'I'm ok thanks, and you?'

She didn't answer me, just started to cry. I sat down on a garden wall, feeling like a complete bastard, I'd done this to her. I thought she was crying because she missed me.

'Don't cry Chrissie.'

Then came the words that flicked a switch in my head. My head felt ready to explode, the red mist began to form.

'He beat me up, Mickey.'

'What?'

'He beat me.'

She carried on crying uncontrollably. My heart felt torn in two listening to her sobs.

'Who beat you?'

'Giles. He kept hitting me and wouldn't stop. I begged and pleaded, but he just ignored me. Are you still there?' she asked, noticing my silence.

'Have you called the police?'

'No, I don't want to.'

'You better call the police Chrissie, for his safety. I'm going to kill him, he's as good as dead.'

'No, I'll call the police in the morning.'

Chrissie went on to tell me what had happened. I think speaking to me seemed to have calmed her down, under the circumstances. I told her to double lock her door and I'd be down on the first train in the morning.

I was mad as hell, full of rage. I just hoped I'd get to Giles before the police did. It was time to take my aggression out on someone or something.

When I left Debbie's house, I had one thing on my mind, pay back. I changed into my combat jacket and balaclava and headed for the Anchor pub, and there it was, AK's black BMW. I started to swing my crow bar. When I'd finished with it, it was unrecognisable. I looked round at the pub windows waiting for someone to come out and confront me, but no one did. All I got was an audience watching through the windows.

That night word got back to AK. He sat in his living room, all his men stood around waiting for him to speak. After about two minutes of angry stares he finally spoke.

'First, you let this fucking action man get away with ninety grand of my money.'

'But they were tooled up AK,' Peanut said.

'You should have seen the armoury they had. We had no chance, we were outnumbered,' Rich added.

'What fucking armoury? Gentleman we are a laughing stock. They were carrying fucking £6.99 toy guns, and as far as being outnumbered, a kid, two slags and a cunt with no legs, are you having a laugh?' AK, raised his voice, 'it's all over Facebook, everyone knows about it apart from you idiots. Now no one wants to buy our weed, because action man and his gang of crack storm troopers are more or less giving it away. So what have you done about it? I'll tell you what you've done about it, fuck all, apart from bricking a window and knocking that slag off her bike. You should have thrown a hand grenade through their front door and blown the fucking house up. Now I hear he's trashed one of our cars. Well the time for playing games is over. I want this cunt dead, and his supplier whoever they are, and I want the weed and my money back.'

'We already know who his supplier is boss.'

They'd been following me for a while, they knew about Giles and my trips to London. They'd seen Giles go to the house and drop off the large black bags full of my stuff. They thought the bags were full of weed. They'd even picked up the business card I threw away outside Naz's shop with the word user written on it. Yes, the stupid bastards thought poor old Giles was my dealer, unluckily for him.

We've got his supplier's name and his address,' Peanut said, as he passed AK the business card.

'This is all very upsetting gents. I don't need this shit. Colin get yourself down to London with Rich. I want to know who this Giles is. I want to know who I'm dealing with and where he gets his stuff, the cheeky cunt, encroaching onto my territory. If he doesn't tell you, beat it out of him. '

'Peanut, Josh, I want you to take care of soldier boy, that guy has got to go, my reputation's at stake here. I want him dead and then find his street rats, I want my ninety grand back and the weed. I don't care how you do it, just get it done. I'm the heavyweight, this is my territory. I'm not losing my title to anybody.'

I arrived back at Debbie's house and let myself in, I needed sleep, it had been a long day. I slept downstairs, just in case we had unwelcome visitors. I sat on the living room sofa in the dark, all I could think about now was Chrissie, and what I was going to do to Giles, the bastard. I was going to make him pay big time.

I checked my phone, Chrissie had texted me *"please tell me you still love me* xx." I replied *"Always xx."*

It was five in the morning, I was hoping to catch the seven o'clock train to London. Before I could do anything else, I needed to see Ash and Daz, to tell them I'd be out of action for a few days.

I left the house and headed for the boat, thinking there'd be no one around this time of the morning, but I was wrong. Unbeknown to me, AK's boys were sat in a van up the road, I was being watched.

I arrived at the boat. Woke Ash and Daz up, and told them I was off down London until the following day. It didn't go down well, with all that was going off. I thought it wise not to tell them about the BMW incident. What they didn't know couldn't hurt them, and it saved me another ear bashing from Daz.

## CHAPTER 22

The train was delayed. I didn't arrive in London until half nine. I walked at a brisk pace towards the exit and down the escalator to my underground platform. When I arrived at Chrissie's flat, I didn't have a clue what to say or expect. She must have watched me walk up the street, because as I got to the door, she pressed the buzzer letting me in. She was standing on the doorstep, I stopped as I got to the top of the stairs, she looked in a terrible state with bruises on her face, but beautiful at the same time. I took a deep breath.

I just stood and stared at her with a half-smile on my face. She put her arms out to me and started to cry. She squeezed me so tight, it felt like she was never going to let me go.

'I've so fucking missed you.'

'I've missed you too.'

I cupped her bruised and battered face between my hands. 'I'm going to kill that bastard for what he's done to you,' I said, kissing her tenderly.

We walked into the living room, I noticed a mirror and her make up on the coffee table. She sat down and began applying a concealing cream in an attempt to hide the damage caused by her boss. By the time she finished, the bruises were no longer visible. For the next couple of hours, we just sat there, we hardly spoke at all, we just cuddled.

'Do you want a coffee?' she asked eventually.

'I'll make it,' I said.

Over the next half hour, she painfully told me what had happened in more detail.

'Since he went up to Derby, to find out who you really were…'

'Did you ask him to go up there?'

'I swear, babe, I didn't know anything about it. When he came back, he was bending over backwards to tell me all about you and who you really were. At first I didn't believe him, then he showed me the pictures of you and your partner, Debbie.'

'She's not my partner.'

'I don't want to know Mickey. Can we leave that for another day?'

Frustrated, I let her carry on. She needed to talk about it.

'He told me all about you, everything, that's when I phoned you. I was gutted. I was in bits, I couldn't work, I couldn't go out of the house. I took it really bad, I started to drink at least two bottles of wine a night. Giles was there for me he was helping me get back on my feet. He started buying me flowers to cheer me up. He came round every night. He told me everything he had was mine, and started saying things like we should be together. He talked me into going out for a meal one night. I said no at first, but he kept asking me until I agreed. I gave in. I was determined to enjoy myself, I wanted a fresh start. We left the restaurant and headed for a wine bar, he was so kind and attentive all evening. We left the bar and walked the short distance to his home, for a coffee. When we arrived at his flat, he opened a bottle of champagne, got down on one knee and asked me to marry him. He offered me a ring and waited for my answer.'

'What happened?'

'I was surprised, but although I was flattered, I turned him down. I know it hurt him. I said to him "Giles I'm really sorry, I don't see you like that, I just see you as a very dear friend." He sat back and snapped closed the case that held the ring. He started to say some really vile things to me, and became violent. I tried to reason with him, but without success. He slapped me a few times before I managed to break away from him, as I ran from the flat, I could hear him screaming at me that I was fired.'

Chrissie's voice started to weaken, I thought she was going to cry. I held her hand tightly. I could tell by her breathing she was finding it painful remembering the events of that night.

'I'm so scared. What if he comes here? He said I was his, he owned me. It was horrible. I spent the next day thinking about what to do. I wanted to phone you straight away, but I couldn't. I nearly phoned the police.'

'You should do. I'm going to go and see him before they get there. That's if there's anything left of him when I've finished.'

'I didn't ask you to come down here to beat him up.'

'Beat him up... I'm going to fucking kill him.'

'Please...'

I'd been there about five hours, when the door buzzer sounded. Chrissie stood up and pressed the button on the intercom.

'Yes, who is it?'

'It's the police, can we have a word, madam.'

Chrissie looked at me, with a look of confusion on her face. She pressed the button to let them in.

'The police, what do they want?' she said.

I got up and dashed towards the bedroom. I had the sinking feeling they were here to arrest me.

'What have you done?'

'Nothing, I just don't like them,' I said. With what I was doing in Derby at the moment, I didn't want to take any chances. I was convinced someone had grassed me up for the weed.

'Don't tell them I'm here ok,' I pleaded, as I shut the bedroom door.

Chrissie open the front door. I heard her say 'how can I help you officers.' I pressed my ear closer to the door so I could hear the conversation clearly.

'Is it alright if we come in, Miss Bryant?'

'What's it about officer?'

'I think it will be best if we came in and explained.'

Chrissie must have let them in, because I heard her ask them to take a seat. I could hear someone coughing, as though they were trying to clear their throat. Then one of the officers spoke.

'You are Chrissie Bryant aren't you?'

'Yes.'

'You work for Giles Cutler, at Retro Fashions?'

'Yes, but why do you need to know that?'

'I'm sorry, I've got some bad news. I'm afraid, Mr Cutler died at eleven o'clock this morning.'

I could imagine Chrissie's expression, she'd be relieved and horrified at the same time. That was the thing with Chrissie, she had a very caring and forgiving nature.

'What... How? I don't believe it. Oh my god...' I heard her say.

'We think he took his own life. I'm afraid we are still investigating the scene as I speak.'

'That's terrible! Why are you informing me?'

'You were listed as an emergency contact number on his mobile. We tracked your address through your phone number.'

The police went on to ask Chrissie a number of questions. The last time she saw him, who his friends were, what his mood was like? Why she decided to take a day off. She didn't tell them he beat her up. The police finished their questioning and got up to leave.

'Thanks for your time Miss, we may be back in touch with you, for further questioning in the future. If we need to, It'll be at the station, are you ok with that?'

'Of course.'

After the police left, I reappeared out of the bedroom, relieved they weren't looking for me.

'That's awful. Giles is dead.'

'I heard everything. Good fucking riddance that's what I say.'

'Don't say that, Mickey.'

'Chrissie, the guy did the right thing.'

'Do you think he did it over me?'

'Don't be silly, and don't you go thinking like that either.'

'They said he jumped from the office window. Giles would never have done that, he loved life too much. Mickey, can I ask you something. I want you to be honest with me was it you, did you kill him?'

'No I was here. You heard the officer, it happened at eleven this morning.'

Then it dawned on me, maybe it wasn't a suicide, had someone thrown him out the window?

'Listen Chrissie, I know it's bad, but I've got to go back to Derby.'

'Why? Don't leave me here all on my own.'

'I have to Chrissie, there's something I have to do. I'll catch the last train to Derby tonight. I promise I'll be back as soon as I can.'

Without my knowledge, at St Pancras station, Colin and Rich were sat in a cafe drinking coffee, it was now late afternoon and very busy. They sat there waiting for the next train going back to Derby. Colin updated AK on their progress.

'It's sorted bro. Mickey's supplier is dead.'

'Fucking hell Colin, I didn't tell you to kill him. I asked you to go down there and see what you could find out.'

'That's what we were trying to do, bro. When we got there he was out of his tree on coke, he wouldn't tell us anything. I hung him out of the window, he still wouldn't talk. He just slipped out of my hands. The coppers will be scraping him up from the pavement, about now.'

Colin ended the call and looked across at Rich.

'Well, that went well, I think.'

'Why, what did he say?'

'Nothing, but he'll have calmed down by the time we get back.'

For most of that evening, I sat cuddled up with Chrissie on her sofa. I couldn't relax, all I could think about was what was happening up in Derby. Chrissie wanted to talk about the future. She told me after what had happened, she didn't want to carry on modelling or have anything to do with the fashion industry. She kept asking what my plans were. I still couldn't tell her anything, I just sat quietly. I knew if I didn't finish the job, there would be no future. It was now half nine, I started to get myself ready.

'What's so important? You don't have to lie anymore. You can tell me. I could come with you.'

'No Chrissie, I need to do this on my own, and anyway, what would it look like to the police, they'd think you'd done a runner. Just lock your door and don't let anyone in. I'll be back as soon as I can.'

I gave her a long hug, kissed her and left her on the doorstep. I looked back at her as I walked down the stairs, she stood there crying. I felt really bad about leaving her on her own, especially with what had just happened, but I had to get back and finish the job I'd started.

I caught my train, grabbed a coffee from the buffet car and sat thinking about what I wanted to do with all the money. The money was for the people I'd leave behind. I knew there was I good chance I wouldn't be coming back, and I wanted to ensure Chrissie and Debbie would be financially secure. I'd already made my mind up months ago. I wanted to swap civilian life in Britain, for the dangers of a war zone. I wanted to go where the fighting was. A few years ago that was Afghanistan, now it was all about ISIS, and I was willing to give them a slap. What really made me want to go there, was a photo I saw on

Facebook of an ISIS fighter holding up the severed head of a woman. It was one of the most, evil things I'd ever seen and it affected me quite a lot. I'd seen a few things in my time, but nothing that compared to that. I'm sure the Kurds would welcome me in their ranks with open arms. Nothing would stop me from going out there, not even Chrissie. Yes, I'd have to let her down again.

While I was on the train heading towards Derby, AK'S henchmen Peanut and Josh were sitting in the car fifty metres away from Debbie's house. At five, past midnight, they saw someone opening the garden gate and disappearing round the back of the house. They got out of the car and followed the shadow to the back of the house towards the shed at the bottom of the garden. The person they were following was Debbie's ex CJ. He'd found out that Debbie was staying at her mum's, and thought he'd take the opportunity to go back and grab his bongs out of the shed, he didn't expect what happened next.

With his box of bongs in his arms, CJ walked out of the shed backwards, turning the light off as he went. Peanut and Josh left him on the ground with his throat slashed from ear to ear.

They didn't bother to wait around to confirm the kill, they knew the cut was that deep it wouldn't take long for him to bleed out. They didn't realize that they had killed the wrong person.

## CHAPTER 23

I arrived in Derby station at around one in the morning, jumped into a taxi and headed straight for The Dogs Bollocks. I just wanted to check that things were ok, I asked the taxi driver to hang around.
The lights were all out. Thinking they were all sleeping, I let myself in. I turned on the dimmer switch slowly, I wasn't expecting to see what I saw next. Daz had been gagged and tied to a chair, his face was nearly unrecognisable, he'd taken one hell of a beating. I started to untie him, he tried to murmur something, but I couldn't understand him. This was all my fault, I thought. I'd let Daz down, if I'd been here this wouldn't have happened.
'You're ok Daz, it's me, you're going to be ok. Who did this?'
I laid him down on the sofa, he tried to speak, but his mouth was too swollen. I helped him drink some water, but he struggled. I needed to know who'd done this to him. He wanted to sit up, so I helped him, then he pointed to a box on his cabinet. It was full of pens and his drawing pad. He pulled out a pen and started to write left handed, he couldn't write with his other hand, they'd hacked two of his fingers off. The writing was just about legible. Daz wrote, *AK MEN.*
'When?' I asked him.
*10 MINS,* he wrote. I asked him where the girls were. *OK HOME,* he scribbled.
'Come on Daz, we've got to get you to A&E.'

I found Daz's missing fingers and put them on ice. I helped him up off the boat and into the waiting taxi.

'Take us to the hospital mate,' I said to the driver.

'What happened to him?' the driver asked, taking a look at Daz.

'He slipped.'

'He needs an ambulance.'

'Just fucking drive, will you.'

I placed a twenty pound note on the dashboard, the driver started the car. In the taxi, Daz managed a few words.

'Said you were dead.'

Ten minutes later we arrived at the hospital, I told the taxi driver to wait. I helped Daz out of the taxi into a wheelchair and pushed him into A&E.

'Excuse me, this my mate Darren Fellows, he's been in a fight and these are his fingers,' I said to the receptionist.

The young female receptionist nearly fainted when I put the two fingers on the reception desk. Seconds later, Daz was on a trolley being carted off. Before they could ask me any questions, I was out and back in the taxi. The car pulled up outside Debbie's house. I paid the driver another twenty pounds, it was his lucky day. I walked up to the house, looking and listening, I knew they were out to get me, I was ready for them.

They told Daz that I was dead. Why would they say that, was it just to scare him? I noticed the side gate was open. Debbie always made sure that the gate was bolted, especially with two kids in the house and playing in the garden. I walked into the garden, something wasn't right.

Fuck, some twat had broken into the shed. The door was wide open and it looked like there was stuff on the path. As

## The Goat Killer

I got closer I realized it was a body, whoever it was had the same combat jacket on as me. I knelt down on one knee, the person was face down, there was a lot of blood. I turned the body to face me. I recognised who it was straight away, CJ, two large bongs lay next to him. I put two and two together. This was why they'd said I was dead. AK's men had thought it was me returning from London. The poor fucker thought he'd risk a kicking, coming back for his bong, he got far more than he bargained for.

Should I just leave the body where it lay and call the police, no that wasn't an option, I'd be prime suspect and be banged up for god knows how long. I'd have to get rid the body, hide it somewhere, but where? It was now gone two in the morning, Derek's allotment that was the only place I could think of. It was about a quarter of a mile away. Could I make it without being seen?

Getting CJ in the wheelbarrow I found in the shed was a nightmare, but I managed it. Five minutes later I was heading for the allotment, I decided to take no chances and went by the long route, through the woods.

I didn't have time to question what I was doing, as far as I was concerned, it was them who had upped the stakes. Once I'd hidden CJ, it was payback time for what they did with Daz and Giles. He certainly needed a kicking, but not being thrown out of a fifth floor window

Peanut and Josh had arrived back at AK's after killing CJ. Colin and Rich sat by the pool. AK stood smiling, looking down at Ash, who'd found himself in a familiar place. He was tied to a metal chair in AK's empty pool. He'd been beaten, but it was minor compared to what Daz had been made to endure.

'We'll have to stop meeting like this, you seem to have taken a liking to my pool. I've got some bad news for you, your friend Mickey sadly passed away about an hour ago, so he won't be around to save your bacon this time.'

'I don't believe you,' Ash replied.

'I'm afraid so. Had his throat cut from ear to ear, and it's your turn next, unless of course you tell me where the rest of the merchandise is.'

Ash remembered what I had told him, tell no one. Under the circumstances, it was probably the best piece of advice I had given.

'I'm not telling you, I'm worth more alive than dead.'

'True. Your father likes his weed doesn't he? Let's say my boys drop by your dad's house. He's in a lot of pain your old man, I hear, on account of him suffering from MS. The weed takes the misery away, I believe. Well out of the kindness of my heart, my boys could do him a big favour and put him out of his misery forever. What do you say?'

'Leave my dad alone, he's done fuck all to you.'

'Did you hear that Colin? It sounds like the boy has come of age, he's grown a pair. Not like the last time you were here, contaminating my pool with your weak bladder. You little shit, tell me where the weed is.'

Ash was determined not to say anymore. AK told Colin and Rich to pay a visit to Ash's, dad's house. Ash had no choice, he knew AK was serious.

'It's hidden on a plot on the allotments in Normanton.'

'Which plot? There's loads of them.'

'The one with an old railway carriage on it, you can't miss it. It's stored inside.'

'Good boy. You see, that didn't hurt did it? I might even keep you alive for a little longer, my dogs have already eaten. By the way, if the weed isn't there, pay a visit to the Ashford's house and collect his dad, so he can join him in the pool. Tyson and Hercules will think it's their birthday.'

I was relieved that the allotment was in sight. It had taken me nearly an hour to travel the short distance. CJ, had fallen off the barrow at least three times. The second time he'd rolled down a bank into someone's back garden. I sat down and rested on the bench me and Derek used to sit on, sharing our stories until it got dark. I bet he's looking down at me right now, laughing his head off. I looked over at CJ, his eyes were open and it looked like he was staring at me.

'What're you looking at, you'll be joining him soon.'

I dragged the body off the barrow and into the carriage, placed him on one of the old chairs, then turned the light on. Derek had everything you could think of in this place, including homemade beer and whiskey, which I sampled once. It near enough blew my fucking head off it was that strong.

I opened a bottle of Derek's beer. It tasted good, just what I needed after lugging CJ around. I sat down next to CJ scratching my head, wondering what to do next. What a fucking mess. I looked around the carriage, there was something missing, the weed. Where was the rest of the gear? While, I was wondering about the whereabouts of the stash, I heard a vehicle, as a precaution I switched the light off.

I pulled the old net curtain to one side and looked out, it was a van. I recognised it straight away. It was AK's men. Peanut got out and started to walk up the track towards the carriage, Josh stayed in his seat. I quickly bolted the door from the inside. I grabbed the first thing I could, a heavy duty shovel, then waited to the side of the door.

The brain dead thug was now looking through the window, but it was too dark to see anything. He tried to open the door, but he couldn't. With a loud bang, the door was kicked in.

He walked in, took a lighter out of his pocket and lit it, he'd come for the weed. The last thing he thought he'd see, was a dead body slumped on a chair in front of him. CJ still had his eyes open, it scared the shit out him.

'What the fuck.'

With precision I swung my shovel and hit him full in the face, he fell to the floor. For good measure, I struck him again on the back of his head, just in case.

'That's for Daz, you bastard.'

He was barely conscious. I sat him next to CJ, and tied him up. I lit a candle. He slowly came round and started to grasp the situation he found himself in.

'Well, isn't this fun?' I said.

'You… I thought we'd killed you,' he replied.

'Nah, I'm afraid not. You killed poor old CJ. He was wearing the same combat jacket as me, to his misfortune.' I looked at his bleeding face, and I thought about Ash. 'I take it you came for the weed? But you got a face full of shovel instead. Where's Ash?'

He said nothing. He just sat there giving me evil looks.

'I'll ask you again, where's Ash? I bet he's at AK's house. Is he still alive? You lot are in the habit of killing people just lately, so I think it's time for a bit of your own medicine, don't you?'

I reached down into a drawer that I knew contained Derek's poultry shears, that he used to prune his plants. I started to gag him. I turned the radio on, to muffle any sound.

'What the fuck are you doing?' he mumbled under the dirty cloth I was stuffing into his mouth.

'Just a little payback for my mate Daz. He'll be so disappointed because he wasn't here to see this.'

I grabbed his hand and cut off of his little finger. His body went rigid with agony. I lowered his gag, he cried and squealed like a baby.

'That's it, let it out. Hurts, doesn't it?'

His screams were drowned out by the loud music coming from the van.

'He's with AK,' Peanut sobbed.

'I know he is.'

I replaced the gag and took his index finger off. The railway carriage was beginning to resemble an abattoir his blood was everywhere. He passed out this time for a few seconds. I slapped his face until he came round. I looked out of the window. Josh was still sat in the van smoking, singing to himself.

'He is into his music, isn't he? If he was any sort of mate, he'd be worried about you by now.'

I decided to make my exit before Josh turned up. I knew where Ash was and that was all that mattered now.

Hopefully he was still alive. I gagged Peanut tightly so he couldn't talk and checked he was tied securely to the chair.

'Sorry mate, I've got to go, hopefully your mate will rescue you soon. I blew out the candle and turned the radio up, it was classic FM, I believe I could fly by R. Kelly was playing. Pretty apt for what was about to happen, with any luck.

Derek always kept two large gas heaters in the carriage for the winter months, the gas canisters were both full. I turned both heaters on to max without igniting them, and left. The idiot in the van didn't see me leave, it was too dark, also he had the cab light on, so he wouldn't see a thing. I waited another five minutes before Josh made a move, he opened the van door and stepped out, leaving the music playing and the engine running. He was doing everything I anticipated. He walked down the track towards the carriage. I slipped into the van.

He pushed open the carriage door, it was now nearly half three in the morning. The radio drowned out the noise of me driving away from the allotment.

Josh fumbled in his pocket for a lighter, at first it wouldn't work then on the third attempt it lit. So did the fucking sky for miles around. Hearing the loud bang, I looked through my rear view mirror. I'm sure I saw Peanut being propelled into space still tied to the chair. The night air was filled with the sound of car alarms going off.

I didn't expect the blast to be as big as that, maybe Derek's five crates of homemade whisky added to the spectacle, cheers Derek.

# CHAPTER 24

I made my way back to Debbie's for a change of clothes, then went to the hospital to check on Daz. I parked up in the car park, it was now gone four in the morning. As I pulled up, a fleet of ambulances left with their lights flashing and sirens wailing away, something big had happened somewhere. I entered A&E, the woman on reception was busy.

'Excuse me, I've come to see how my buddy is.'

'Name?'

'Darren Fellows.'

'Just a moment.'

I ignored her and went through to where the emergency cubicles were. I was confronted by a nurse.

'Can I help you, sir?'

'I'm looking for my buddy Darren Fellows, he lost some fingers.'

'If you take a seat, I'll find out where he is for you.'

The nurse returned with an upset looking Debbie. I expected a barrage of abuse from her. She'd been against Daz being involved in my plan, so I knew she'd blame me.

'He's just come out of surgery after having his fingers sewn back on, it looks like the operation was successful. You can't see him now, he'll be sedated. Come back tomorrow,' the nurse said.

'Thanks,' I said, at least he was alright, that's what I wanted to hear.

The nurse walked away, leaving me alone with Debbie.

'What the hell's been going on? Is this all AK's doing? Are you ok Mickey?'

'I'm fine. I've got to go, there's something I have to do. Give the kids a big hug from their uncle Mickey. I can't explain right now Deb's, I'm sorry.'

'I might as well fucking wait here, then. You'll be next or even worse, I'll have to go down the undertakers. I know where you're going. Let the police deal with AK.'

Debbie started to cry. I hated the fact that my actions had caused this mess. As I walked away, I heard a lot of commotion coming from two of the other cubicles.

'Yes, both have first and second degree burns. This one has two fingers missing.'

'What another one? Do we have the fingers?'

'I'm afraid not doctor.'

I walked down the corridor and out of the main exit back to the van. I drove back to Debbie's house, it was now half four, it would be light in an hour. I went straight to the shed, I had to clean up the blood, so there was no trace anywhere. Luckily, most of CJ's blood had trickled into the soil, I dug it over just in case, and scrubbed the path until there was no visible sign of any blood. I made myself a coffee and planned my next move. I knew where Ash was, hopefully he was still alive.

I knew they would be expecting Peanut and Josh back, so getting in AK's hopefully wouldn't be a problem. Piece of cake then. I got myself tooled up as much as I could, a carving knife and baseball bat, not much good against bullets, but I had the element of surprise and that was crucial. I put on my gloves I had my balaclava in my pocket and I was ready.

## The Goat Killer

There was one last thing I had to do, that was visit my brother Matt. Matt didn't mind me visiting him whatever time of day it was. I arrived at the cemetery with my usual two cans of beer and placed them down on his grave. He'd been killed by the IED that took Daz's legs. I got down on one knee.

'I know you wouldn't have approved of what I'm about to do, but even when you were alive you could never stop me, so nothing changes eh. I know you'll be looking down on me, watching my back. I've never told you this, but you were the best brother I could ever have and if I end up there with you, I couldn't think of a better place. Man, we'd have one hell of a party, so whatever happens, so be it, I love you, bro.'

I got back into the van with a tear in my eye, I was so up for this.

My sombre mood changed when I saw Peanut's two fingers on the van floor under the glove compartment, they must have fallen out of my pocket when I got into the van. I wanted to keep them to show to Daz, a sort of trophy, he'd love that, but I thought of a better use for them. I reached down to pick them up, as I turned my head, I looked up, and taped under the glove compartment I found a fully loaded 9mm pistol, I pulled it off. Well, well, the element of surprise and a bit of hardware. Matt must have heard me. He was looking down on me already.

I drove to AK's. I didn't really have any sort of plan, what was going to happen, would happen. I approached the gates and waited for them to open. they didn't open at first, then I flashed the headlights and as if by magic I was in. My heart was now pumping.

AK stood beside the nearly half full pool. The water was up to Ash's shoulders.

'Please let me go, I've told you all you want to know,' the boy pleaded.

'If this van is full of weed and the rest of my money, you might be in luck son.'

'Shall I turn the water off?' Lisa asked, looking concerned, hovering behind him.

He ignored her and instructed Rich to see what was taking Peanut and Josh so long. They should have appeared from the garage by now, with the news he was hoping for. By this time, I was standing to one side of the garage door, the two Rottweilers were sat in front of the van, happily chewing away on Peanuts fingers. I'd given them to the dogs to keep them quiet.

The garage door opened and Rich entered. The look of confusion on his face was replaced with a look of surprise, when he felt the cold metal of my gun placed to the side of his head.

'Don't say a fucking word or you're a dead man. Turn around and walk out of the door.'

Rich walked back out of the door and towards the pool, with the gun still firmly held to his head. We walked towards AK, who was in the middle of an argument with Lisa, she had blood coming from her mouth.

'Don't you question me bitch, the water is staying on.'

'I told you before AK, if you ever hit me again, it would be the last time.'

'What you going do? What the fuck are you going to do? Tell me.'

We walked out of the semi-darkness into the pool lights, Rich announced my arrival. AK looked round, he looked surprised to see me.

'You... what the fuck?'

'I'm a fucking ghost. I came back to haunt you.'

'Where's Peanut and Josh?'

'They're ok. We had our own firework party, you missed it. It was spectacular too.'

By now Ash was struggling to keep his head above water. He had to revert to breathing through his nose.

'Turn the fucking water off now, you, sick fuck,' I shouted as I stood beside the pool.

Lisa made a move to towards the tap, which was at the back of the house.

'Stay where you are, Lisa,' he said in a menacing voice.

'Fuck you.'

AK then grabbed hold of her, dragging her back by her hair.

'Let go of me.'

The situation got more complicated when Colin appeared from the house, brandishing a shotgun.

'This is fun isn't it? Why don't we all calm down and try to sort this out,' he said.

With Colin's shotgun trained on me, and my gun trained on Rich, and Ash about to drown, something was telling me this was going to end badly. Ash was more or less under water, desperately trying to grab gulps of air.

'Aren't you going to save your friend, Mickey? You're not going to let him die are you?'

'Get in there and untie him,' I said to Rich, as I prodded him in the back with the gun.

'Fuck you,' Rich replied.

I pushed him into the pool at the deep end, then trained my gun on AK. Rich started to struggle and splash around like an octopus having a fit.

'What's up with him?' I asked.

'He can't, fucking swim, that's what's up with him,' Colin said.

I had no choice, Ash was drowning. I jumped into the pool, and dived under the water. I pulled out my knife and cut Ash free, then dragged him to the surface of the pool. In my hurry to rescue the boy, I'd dropped the 9mm pistol I held.

The gang boss was now sitting down giving me a slow hand clap. I knew then I was fucked.

'Wow! You're one fucking hero, you are,' he said

I climbed out of the pool and pulled Ash out; he lay motionless, but breathing. I looked over at Rich, who was by now losing the fight to stay above water and drowning. I made a move to go back in the pool to save him, but I was struck to the floor with a blow from the butt of Colin's shotgun. I came to a few minutes later. I'd just about got my bearings, when I felt yet another blow to my head, this time it was his brother's boot. With blood pouring down my face, Colin grabbed me by my arms and sat me down in a patio chair facing AK. Ash lay to one side still unconscious.

'You know, all this could have been avoided, if you'd taken my offer and worked for me,' he said

'It all could have been avoided if you hadn't tried to rip me off,' I answered defiantly.

Then came a slap from him, one of many.

'I didn't ask you to speak soldier boy, shut the fuck up. You have truly messed everything up. All because you got involved in something you know fuck all about. I bet you're regretting it now, soldier boy. I'll ask you once and you'd better give me the answer I want, or you won't like what's next.' He signalled to his brother, who headed in the direction of the house.

His face was now one inch away from my bloodied face.

'Where's my money and the merchandise?'

I looked away, anticipating the blow to my face that was about to come my way. I was right. Colin now had me in a headlock, I couldn't see, my eyes were filled with blood. I felt AK forcing my mouth open, then I felt something around two of my front teeth, then he pulled, the pain was unbearable. I tried to stifle the scream that broke from my lips. Ash was now awake and looking on. Knowing he was ok, was of little comfort, given the situation.

'Unless you start talking, I'll take all your teeth out, one by one.'

I said nothing. I hadn't got a clue where the weed was anyway.

'Tell him Mickey,' Lisa pleaded. I don't think she liked the idea of torture.

'Sounds like you've got an admirer; I'd listen to her if I were you Mickey.'

He walked forward again and took another tooth. Lisa looked away.

'Fuck me, you're either a brave son of a bitch or stupid. Isn't he brave Lisa? They usually talk after the first tooth. Dentistry is so expensive nowadays and it's really hard to get it done on the national health. Don't worry Mickey, I won't charge you for this.'

After the third extraction I'd given up, I just wanted the pain to end. He was going to kill us both anyway, that was obvious. All I could do was buy us some time.

'It's in the back of the van.'

'Don't fucking lie to me,' he shouted as he hit me again.

'Go and check the van,' he said nodding at Colin, 'If you're lying to me, you, cunt, I'm going to let my dogs rip you apart.'

Colin walked off towards the van, I knew I only had minutes before I joined my brother Matt.

'Lisa, go and get the dogs.'

'No. This has gone too far.'

'I said go and get the dogs. Now!'

'They're my dogs as well. I'm not letting you do it.'

AK walked up to the woman and slapped her face hard. The force of the blow made her stumble.

'Get the fucking dogs, bitch.'

Colin looked back in anger at his brother, as Lisa followed him to the garage where the dogs were kept.

'You see Mickey, that's how you treat women. You've got to keep them under control.'

I could hear the van doors open, that was it, I'd just signed my death warrant. I had to do something before they got back, but there was nothing I could do, I was tied to a chair. AK had his gun pointing straight at me, and I was too weak to make any attempt to rescue the situation. This time

## The Goat Killer

for the first time in my life, I'd given up. I'd given it my best shot. I thought of Chrissie and what could have been... and then something strange happened.

'It's there.'

'What?'

'The money and the weed. It's all in the back of the van,' Colin shouted.

AK looked at me and smiled. If you ever saw him smiling you'd know how unnerving it was.

'You're having me fucking on,' he said.

I grinned, then I wondered if this was one of my fucking dreams. Any moment now I'll wake up next to Chrissie, in a nice warm bed with all my problems gone away.

'I don't believe you. There's no way he would sit there and go through that for no reason, unless he's some sort of nutter,' AK said.

'See for yourself, it's all there,' Colin called out.

He untied me, pulled me up from the chair and we walked to the van. What was going on? That bang on the head must have done some damage, this wasn't making sense. We all entered the garage and walked to the back of the van. AK climbed in the back and looked around.

'Jokes over, where's is it? There's fuck all in this van. Will someone tell me what the fuck is going on?'

To be honest, I was thinking the same thing. I knew the weed hadn't been there when I arrived at the house.

'I'm sorry AK,' Lisa said, tearfully.

Colin pointed his shotgun at AK at point blank range, fired and blew the top of his head off. It was just like the top coming off a boiled egg.

'Don't just stand there. Give me a hand,' Colin said, looking at me.

What was happening, I didn't have a clue. I was just glad to be alive.

# CHAPTER 25

A few months later in Malaga, Chrissie was sitting by the pool reading the Spanish Sun. Tears stream down her cheeks as she reads an article. There's a picture of me in uniform underneath the headline, which reads, *Army Veteran brings down drugs gang, is hailed as a hero. Tributes have been paid to army Veteran Michael Saunders 30 from Derby. He was killed on the 13 of September, after coming to the rescue of one of his students, from the college where he worked as a security officer. The young male student, who can't be named, asked the security officer for help after he'd been threatened by a local drugs gang. Then a few days later, Michael received information that the young student had been kidnapped, and was being held at a certain location in Derbyshire. Mr Saunders, on his own, entered the property where the student was being held. The student was tied up in a swimming pool. After rescuing the student, a number of shots were fired and a house fire broke out at the property. Following the coroner's report, we can now confirm that two bodies found at the premises were those of gang leader Tommy Gamble and gang member Richard Best. It has also been confirmed, that the remains of Michael Saunders, were found in an incinerator used for the cremation of pets. Mr Saunders ex-girlfriend said, "Mickey was the nicest and most honest man I'd ever met. He served two tours in Afghanistan and on his last tour, he survived an IED, but spent six months in hospital in Birmingham, his best friend lost two limbs and his brother lost his life. What Mickey did doesn't surprise me, he was always willing to help others whatever the situation."*

*Police Inspector Rogers from the Derbyshire Police said, "Mr Saunders was a courageous and brave man, and his memory will live on for a long time, but we strongly recommend that you should always contact the police if you find yourself in a similar situation."*

Chrissie lowered her paper and looked out to sea. She patted her eyes with a tissue.

'He was a hero after all, my hero.'

It makes you want to burst into tears doesn't it? Let me tell you what really happened next.

We carried AK and Rich's bodies into the house using plastic sheeting, so there was no blood trail. We laid them both down in the living room a few yards apart, placing an AK47 in AK's hands and the used shotgun in Rich's. To make things more convincing, Colin had fired a shot into Rich with the AK47.

'It's your lucky day, Mickey,' Lisa said looking at me, 'don't worry, me and Colin had planned this a while back, you just made it easier for us. With you getting Peanut, Josh and now Rich out of the way, all that was left was AK.'

'Hold on a minute, are you two an item?' I asked.

'Yes, brother or no brother, he'd hit Lisa once too often. That was the last time,' Colin said.

'But what about all this?' I asked, indicating the house and gardens.

'What? This is just a crime scene now. We're moving on, I suggest you and Ash do the same. The police will be

## The Goat Killer

swarming all over this place soon. After the gunshots, someone's bound to report it. The police will come to the conclusion that this was just another gangland bust up. We're taking the van, along with the dogs and the plastic sheeting. The only other evidence is AK's brains splattered inside the van and gunshot residue.'

Lisa was busy pouring a can of petrol all over the house, Colin was helping himself to the contents of the safe.

'We've taken what we need out of there, what's left is yours if you want it. If you hurry up, we'll give you a lift into Derby.'

'I don't need a lift, just go. I can finish off here,' I said, glad to be alive.

Colin and Lisa drove away. I filled a bin bag with what was left in the safe. It looked like there was enough money in there to do what I wanted to do. I placed my four extracted teeth in my pocket. I quickly grabbed the bag of cash and lit the fire.

Ash was sitting up by the pool, he'd vomited, but he was ok. I could hear the police sirens in the distance, it wouldn't be long before they were here.

'Come on Ash, we're going.'

Ash had just about come to his senses, but he was in no condition to go anywhere.

'No, you go. I know what to say to the police, honest. Thanks for saving me mate.'

I had no choice, I had to leave. I gave Ash a hug and promised I'd see him right.

'See you again soon. Ash. Take care,' I said, and with that I was gone.

I quickly jogged down the path, to the chapel AK had shown me on my first visit. I'd found the perfect way to disappear. I opened the door and headed to the area where the incinerators were. Opening the door of the first incinerator, I found it full of ashes. I took the teeth from my pocket, threw them in and brushed some of the ashes over them. I closed the door and set the timer for five minutes, then switched it on. Getting off the property was easy, AK had thoughtfully shown me the back entrance, used by grieving pet owners.

I had the money I needed, I could do what I wanted to do, be where I wanted to be. I headed straight to Debbie's house, grabbed most of my gear and left. Once I was out the country, my plan was to contact a YPG recruiter (Kurdish People's Protection Units) and within weeks I'd be on a plane on my way to Iraq. Where I'd would be picked up by Kurdish rebels and smuggled by land into Syria.

Lying with all my equipment and M16 rifle next to me, I was waiting for the call, I was off over the border. I was to join the growing influx of foreign freedom *fighters,* helping Kurdish forces destroy Daesh in Syria.

Many soldiers who leave their country's armed forces eventually make the difficult transition into civilian life. Some never quite get there, ending up depressed, druggies and on the streets. Then there are a few of us who miss the adrenaline and glamour of battle, that was me. I was in a happy mood.

My dream didn't last long. I was awoken by Chrissie. I was laying on my bed in Spain. The place I'd been dreaming about you see, was where I originally wanted to be. Meeting up with Chrissie the night after the death of AK, changed my mind instantly, when she revealed she was pregnant. I was going to be a father, this stopped me in my tracks. My place was there with Chrissie and my soon to be born son.

The dreams had stopped. My bloodthirsty, adrenaline junkie days were behind me. With the money I stole from AK, the future we had talked about a few years ago could happen. Chrissie will get her clothes shop. I will have my own bar.

Back in England my funeral went ahead, my remains, (my four teeth) were buried in the same plot as my brother Matt. Everyone was there, the ones who thought I was dead, and the ones who knew I was very much alive, Debbie, Daz and Ash.

# EPILOGUE

## The Alibi

Ash did a brilliant job convincing the police his version of events was true. That he was being made to deal drugs at the college, and if he didn't they beat him. He couldn't go to the police for fear they'd hurt his dad, so he confided in and asked me for protection. Then he got kidnapped and tortured, I found out where he was and saved him. He told them he didn't know what happened after that, he was unconscious. Having found my blood on the chair and paving beside the pool, they swallowed the whole story.

## The Missing Weed

Thinking that AK was closing in on the weed, Ash and Steph moved the weed to her flat just in case, using Steph's brother's van. With the money he made in the summer from his job on the side, he plans to go on to university in September, he wants to become a botanist.

## Peanut and Josh

After surviving the fireworks display, Peanut and Josh were charged with murder. The knife that was used to kill CJ was still in Josh's pocket. The police said that they'd kidnapped CJ, and taken him to the allotment where they intend to kill him, then dispose of his body in the ground, after a fresh half dug hole was discovered nearby.

## Colin and Lisa

Colin was wanted in connection with the murder of Giles. He and Rich were identified by CCTV camera, entering Giles's premises at the time of his death. Colin and Lisa were both also wanted for questioning in relation to the deaths of AK, Rich and myself, they are still on the run.

## Debbie and Daz

Daz managed to save his fingers and was happy living with Debbie and her kids. He sold The Dogs Bollocks. They plan to get married next year, then move house to the countryside.

## Dave Sherwood

It was established three months later, that Sherwood had been talking on his mobile at the time of the accident.

## Facts

The illicit trade in cannabis stretches from some of the poorest countries on Earth to middle-class homes in the UK. It is now believed to be the biggest source of income for organized crime gangs around the world.

The global cannabis trade is reckoned by the United Nations Office on Drugs and Crime to be worth a staggering £200 billion a year.

The Goat Killer

Printed in Great Britain
by Amazon